THE END
IS
THE BEGINNING

THE END
IS
THE BEGINNING

Helene Conway

Jacket Painting by Dave Palladini

 Follett Publishing Company / Chicago

ISBN 0-695-40241-2 Titan binding
ISBN 0-695-80241-0 Trade binding

Library of Congress Catalog Card Number: 77-161554

First Printing

For My Sister Mary

INTRODUCTION

The first Anglo-Norman knights came to Ireland in the twelfth century to assist one Irish king in his quarrel with another. But, they did not leave, when the quarrel was over, as would have been the Irish way. Instead, having gained a foothold, they stayed on as conquerors, as the Normans had been doing for a century in many parts of Europe.

Because their coats of mail gave them superiority in battle, the knights assumed that the way of life, language, and law of the Gaelic Irish were inferior to their own. The English kings claimed the title of Lord of Ireland, but for many years could impose their will effectively only on the coast across from England. As their own subjects moved away from that coast, many were inclined to intermarry with the Gaels, adopt their customs, and govern by their laws.

When Henry VII, the first Tudor king, had established himself as a despot in England, he turned his attention to Ireland. One of his first moves, in 1494, was to proclaim English law the law of Ireland. This placed in jeopardy all land titles held under Gaelic law and was frequently used to give an air of legality to the seizure of Irish land for the English.

The separation of England from the Church of Rome in 1534 deepened the antipathy between the two islands, for most of the Irish and the English in Ireland remained faithful to the Catholic religion. Under the Tudor kings, too, began the uprooting of all Irish peasants from sections of the land and the "planting" of English in their place. When the Stuart dynasty followed the Tudors, O'Neill and O'Donnell, the two great Earls of Ulster (Northern Ireland), fled the country in 1607 rather than obey a summons to the court of James I, which, they feared, meant imprisonment. The king, in accordance with English law, though contrary to Irish law, claimed all their lands and sold them to Englishmen and Scotsmen, who were Protestant. Later, when Oliver Cromwell subdued Ireland, he moved many of the Irish still in Ulster to other places and "planted" more English there, bringing the number of Protestant settlers to 100,000.

James I also encouraged the recruitment of Irishmen for armies on the continent of Europe. For many, made landless by the "plantations," this offered a way of life more acceptable than remaining in Ireland. Oliver Cromwell permitted the Irish generals he defeated to emigrate with their troops. 34,000 are said to have left Ireland between 1652 and 1654. Others, however, remained in Ireland, living outside the law, in caves, or in cabins hidden deep in woods and glens. From these they sallied forth to administer their own brand of justice to the settlers. They were called "rapparees," from a Gaelic word meaning "half-stick," because of their dexterity in taking their muskets apart and using the barrel as an innocent looking walking stick, when possession of a firearm would be dangerous. When Charles II was restored to the English throne, in 1660, a few of the men who had emigrated, returned. To some who had supported him, Charles gave back the land which had been taken from them under Cromwell.

There was rejoicing in Ireland when Charles was succeeded by his brother James II, for the latter was a convert to the Catholic faith. But Protestant England feared a Catholic king, and invited his son-in-law, William of Orange (part of modern Holland), to take the throne. Deserted by most of his English subjects, James fled to the protection of Louis XIV of France.

The king's viceroy in Ireland, Tyrconnell, refused to acknowledge William as king. With the exception of Ulster, the majority of Irishmen, whether of Gaelic, Norman, or English blood, were with Tyrconnell. In March of 1689, King James landed at Dublin, with arms and ammunition from the French king. The following year, William landed with reinforcements for his army in the north. Their two armies met at the Boyne. William, with 36,000 men and superior firepower, defeated the 23,000 men under James' banner. The defeated Irish retreated towards Limerick, while James returned to France.

It was then that Patrick Sarsfield, son of an Anglo-Irish family, who had fought in Spain and England for the Stuart kings, held the defeated Irish together. William laid seige to Limerick, but was driven back and took his army into winter quarters in Ulster. In the spring, the Dutch general, Ginkel, led that army south again and, fording the Shannon at Athlone, met the Irish army at Aughrim. Sarsfield had urged the French commander, St. Ruth, to battle the superior English force in the traditional Irish way of dodging movement. St. Ruth insisted on a pitched battle. As he was leading a charge, he was beheaded by an English cannonball. Because of St. Ruth's death, Sarsfield with the calvary reserve, was not called into the battle. All he could do was save the remnants of the defeated army falling back on Limerick, which was soon under siege for the second time.

There were still, however, armed bands of rapparees roaming the countryside. Many of these men had enlisted in King James's army and fought at the Boyne and Aughrim. Refusing to be walled up in the besieged city, they now returned to their old free way of life. From time to time they came out of their hiding places, to wreak their vengeance on those whom they considered traitors to Ireland. Then they retreated again into their caves, as if the earth had swallowed them.

CHAPTER ONE

Owen's eyes opened to the darkness of his room. It was not a dream. Real hoofbeats were coming up the avenue. He jumped out of bed and rushed to the window which overlooked the approach to the house. The gray mist was like a blanket outside the glass. It muffled the sound which seemed for a moment directly below him. He went to the side window where he could hear the hoofbeats again. They were heading for the stable. First opening his door quietly, he ran down the hall to the window at the back. Here he could see the outline of the stable roofs, but the yard was shrouded in mist. He heard the faint creak of leather, as if riders were dismounting, but no voices reached his ears. Then sharp and clear came a whistle, like a curlew's call. The birdlike cry sounded a second time; then there was silence as thick as the fog in the stable yard.

Owen ran back to his room, glad that his bare feet made no sound on the thick carpet, for he did not want to wake his mother. He began to pull on his clothes. He must find out what was going on. Why, he wondered, had not Brian barked. Then Owen realized who the visitors must be. The rapparees! And Patrick was expecting them. Otherwise the wolfhound's bay would have sounded before the horsemen had reached the stable yard.

Owen recalled what Patrick had said one day, a few weeks ago, as he was saddling Donegal, the last hunter left in the Cloona stables: "Don't ride out on the high road, Master Owen. A passing soldier, be he Irish or English, might take the horse from you. Keep to the lanes and the tracks."

"But mightn't I run into the rapparees there?"

His head bent to tighten the saddle's girth, Patrick had replied, "Never you worry about the rapparees, lad. You've no better friends than 'those lawless men' as your mother calls them. Though you'd not find them friendly if you tried to approach them. Should you see any, and I doubt they'll let you, just go your way and they'll go theirs."

That warning recalled, Owen decided it was better not to go dashing out to the stable yard in the middle of the night. For though this was the first time he had heard any riders, he had been sure that Patrick was in touch with the rapparees. Where else would he get news of the siege, which otherwise came only when the west wind carried the boom of the distant guns around Limerick.

When Owen awoke next morning, a westerly wind was blowing away the night mist, but even when he opened his window to the cool October air, he could hear no sound of guns. After dressing quickly, he hurried out to the stable where he found Patrick grooming Donegal.

"'Tis early you're out this morning, Master Owen."

"I don't hear the guns. I thought you might know why."

"And how would that be, that I'd know why they stopped fighting twenty miles away?"

"There were horsemen here last night. I heard—"

"You heard nothing."

Owen backed away from the stern look and almost-threatening tone. This was a different Patrick from the kind man who had served the Bourkes as long as Owen could remember.

"Now, then, lad." Patrick's face cleared and his voice was soft. "I shouldn't have spoken that way. But you must never hear anything at night. That's important. While I'm here, no harm can come to you and your mother. Now, I want your promise that you'll not mention what you heard, or thought you heard, last night to anyone."

"I promise, Patrick, but I only thought there might be word from—"

"Now you're not to think how that might come," Patrick interrupted. "I'd best go with you to your mother. And I'll tell you nothing until we are with her."

They walked across the cobbled yard, through the big kitchen, and into the dining room, where Owen's mother sat at breakfast. Anna, the English maid who had been with her since her marriage, was serving the morning meal.

"I've news you should hear, Mistress Bourke," Patrick

began, "though it's nothing to make your heart glad this fine morning."

Mrs. Bourke put down the cup she had been holding. "We're used to bad news, Patrick. What is it now?"

Patrick cleared his throat. "They say the fighting has stopped and articles of surrender are being drawn up. Sarsfield will be allowed to take the army to France, they do say, but what's to become of the rest of us there's no telling."

Owen heard her quick intake of breath, but in a moment his mother spoke calmly enough. "Is that all you've heard, Patrick?"

"They do say that the treaty will be signed today. The cavalry have been allowed to join the other troops in the city and weren't the leaders at dinner with the Dutch general, Ginkel, yesterday. And him our mortal enemy! Surrender and take the army to France is what they plan, I hear. When there's anything more, I'll bring it to you. But you'll likely be hearing from Mr. Richard himself soon."

"Thank you, Patrick. I've no doubt we will, but meanwhile I rely on you to keep me informed." The little smile she gave Patrick as he turned to leave assured Owen that she too had heard the horsemen in the night.

"Do you think Uncle Richard will go to France with the army?" Owen asked. "And what will we do?"

"I feel sure your uncle will go. As to what we will do, we'd better have breakfast now. Anna, you may bring in Master Owen's."

"Please, ma'am, I hope you'll be taking the boy and yourself back to your parents in England now, away from this wild country where there's never an end of fighting."

"Hush, Anna. This is a fine country that I'll be content to stay in, if we're allowed. England is no better for those of us who hold to the Catholic religion and the Stuart king. It's no place for Owen to grow up in. I pray that we may remain here and hold our land at Cloona, as his father would have wished."

As Anna went into the kitchen, still muttering about the wild Irish land to which fifteen years had not reconciled her, Owen asked, "Do you think Uncle Richard will come here before he goes to France?"

"I'm sure he will, if he can. When he does, we will know better what the future holds."

"And if he thinks we should go to France with him?" Owen persisted, knowing that his mother might not take Richard's advice.

"I don't know, Owen. So much depends on the terms of the treaty. Until we know what they are, it is useless to plan. If it's at all possible to stay here, I—that's what your father would wish—" Her voice broke as she turned her face away.

Owen knew that she was right. He recalled what his father had said before he had ridden away to battle, never to return: *The Irish have wasted their strength fighting in foreign lands, Owen. I pray God we have enough left to save our own. Whatever happens to me, stay with the land, if you can, my son.*

But there was little left to hold on to, Owen thought. A few fields and the one stretch of woods were all that was left of Cloona, the once wide estate of the Bourkes.

Only Anna and Ellie the cook in the kitchen and Patrick and Gavin, the stable boy, in the stables. Only a few old men were left with the women and children in the village. What kind of life would there be here, if the men now in the army went to France? Owen wondered if his mother were thinking the same thoughts as, her composure regained, she rose from her chair. Owen was relieved, for neither of them had much appetite. Further discussion was pointless. Until Uncle Richard came, no decision could be made.

Following his mother into the hall, Owen wished that she would release him from the two hours of study which daily followed breakfast. Instead she turned before going upstairs to say, "I'll be down in an hour for your French lesson."

Owen went into the study behind the drawing room and sat at the desk, thinking, not for the first time, that his mother did not understand how a boy of thirteen felt. Had his father or uncle been there, they would have known his need to gallop down the lanes on Donegal or race with Brian through the fields. Impatiently he opened "Le Cid," but he could not keep his mind on what he was reading. His thoughts kept returning to the conversation with Patrick that morning. He remembered the words, *While I'm here, no harm can come to you and your mother.* Surely Patrick, alone, could do little to protect them in any real danger. Of course, it was his link with the rapparees that had kept them safe so far. That was why Donegal had not been stolen, nor Cloona looted by wandering soldiers, or rapparees for that matter. Owen smiled, remembering how his mother had denounced those men who led their hidden lives close to but yet apart from the other villagers. That might be his future if he and his mother stayed at Cloona, Owen thought. She would not care for that. Nor would she like it if he stumbled over the three pages of Corneille's tragedy which she would soon be coming to hear him read. He picked up the book, forcing himself to keep his mind on the printed page. If he did go to France, he would be glad that his mother had taught him French. It was as familiar to her as English, for her family had fled to France during Cromwell's time, and she had remained there until her marriage.

Patrick had been wrong about the signing of the treaty, he confessed the next morning—although Owen had heard no sound of horsemen in the night.

" 'Twas only a suspension of arms," Patrick explained. "They've stopped fighting and begun haggling over terms. Though little good they'll be when all the young men have gone to France and there's no one left to make the English keep the treaty. But I'd not say that in front of your mother."

"And why not?" Owen asked as he followed Patrick out of the stable, where he had been pitching hay.

"You'll not be forgetting she's English."

"But she holds to the Stuart king. You don't think she has any sympathy with those who follow the Orangeman?" Owen asked.

"That I don't, lad. But it's a cruel sorrow to her that

they are her countrymen. I've seen pain in her eyes when they're spoken of. I'd not be the cause of it."

Owen was ashamed that Patrick had observed what he had not. "Do you think Uncle Richard will come soon?" he asked, to change the subject.

"Not before the treaty is signed. None may leave the city till then."

How long would that be, Owen wondered, impatient for his uncle's coming. The daily routine at Cloona seemed unbearably dull. There was no longer even the excitement of galloping over the open roads to relieve the tedium. His daily rides on Donegal served to exercise the horse, but that was all.

On the last day of October, after returning Donegal to the stable, Owen wandered restlessly around the house and down the avenue of oak trees that led to the gate. Then he heard the sound of hoofbeats coming from the river road that followed the Shannon from Limerick. He waited until horse and rider came into sight. It was Uncle Richard. Owen flung open the gate. After getting down from the saddle, Richard threw his arm around Owen. "It's good to find you waiting for me, Owen, but how did you know that I'd be coming today?"

"I didn't. But, oh! It's good to see you. I began to wonder if you'd ever come."

"Surely you never doubted that."

"It's been so long."

"Yes, a long weary time, for me as well as for you. But

I see your mother at the door. She'll not want us to linger here."

As they walked together up the avenue, Patrick came limping towards them. "Well, Mr. Richard," he said, as he took the reins to lead the horse off to the stable, "I suppose you'll be leaving soon, now that the French ships have arrived."

"Yes, I'll be going within the week."

They were at the door now, and Richard took his arm from Owen's shoulders as he stepped forward to greet his sister-in-law. Owen noticed then how thin his uncle looked. There were brown stains on his red coat, and his leather boots were unpolished. He was no longer the gay cavalier who had come home from France to liberate Ireland. He walked slowly through the hall and into the study behind Mrs. Bourke. When he sat down, he sighed and closed his eyes. There were lines on his face that had not been there before.

"So, this is the end, Richard." Margaret Bourke's voice was full of compassion.

"That I will not believe." His vehemence erased the weary lines from his face. "Though we go to France, we will return, I swear it."

"Oh, Richard, can you still have hope? Two years ago, I believed, too, when you came back from France and James rode out so confidently, never to return." Tears shone in her eyes. "Surely with this defeat, we must accept the fact that William will rule here, as he does in England, and the Stuart king will not return."

"I'll not argue the point," Richard said almost cheerfully. "I'd be sorry to hear you speak this way if it did not make my task easier. I want you to come to France with me. I could not feel easy leaving you at Hugh's mercy, yet I must go."

"Cousin Hugh?" Owen asked. "What has he to do with us? Won't he be going with the army, too?"

"Not he." Richard's face was stern. "He's the only Bourke I ever heard of who turned traitor."

"Richard!" Margaret Bourke's voice was sharp. "He was here after the battle at Aughrim. He stopped to see that all was well with us before joining his troops in Limerick."

"That was his story. Seeing to the well-being of his 'dear relatives' gave him his excuse for leaving his regiment. From here he went straight to the English camp."

Owen clenched his fists. "If I had known—"

Richard patted his nephew's shoulder. "What's one traitor more or less? There will be plenty of others going over to William's side when they feel our cause is hopeless."

"And isn't it?" Margaret asked quietly.

"It will be many months before that is decided," Richard replied. "Meanwhile, will you come to France? That must be decided now."

"Now? This minute?"

"By tomorrow morning."

"But surely, Mother," Owen said, "there can be but one answer. You won't stay here if you believe the struggle is lost."

It was to Richard that his mother turned. "You have told us so little. What are the terms of the treaty? Will all estates still in Irish hands be confiscated? Is Cloona lost to us?"

Richard went over to the hearth and stood facing the room, his arm resting on the mantle shelf. "Ten thousand men will follow Sarsfield to France—"

"Oh! No! What will happen to their families?"

"Please, Margaret, hear me out. The English have agreed to provide ships to take their families and household goods, the infantry, that is. The cavalry, with their families, will go in the French ships which arrived too late to help us at the siege. We will sail soon and I want you to come with me." He raised his hand to forestall another interruption. "Under the terms of the treaty Catholics will have the same privileges in the exercise of their religion as they had under Charles II and, if they take the oath of allegiance to William and Mary, may hold their estates under the same conditions as applied under Charles."

As his mother considered these words, Owen exclaimed, "Mother you could not take such an oath. Father would never—"

"Please, Owen! If your father were here, he would go with the army and we, of course, would go with him. But without him—to go into exile, to be dependent upon the bounty of others—I must have time to think. I cannot toss aside your inheritance lightly. It would be forfeited if we went, wouldn't it?" she asked Richard.

"Undoubtedly! But think of this, Margaret. Hugh is in the English camp. He may well claim Cloona as his reward for going over. You know, as well as I do, how easy it is to find a flawed title to an Irish estate. Think what the future here may hold. It could be worse than the bitterness of exile. In France I could still look after you as James asked me to do."

"It will not be an easy decision, Richard. There is so much at stake. You will have my answer in the morning. Now I must see that your room is made ready for you."

Owen wanted to speak, to tell his mother how very much he wanted to go to France. Surely she would like to return to that country where she had lived as a girl, where she had met and married his father. With surprise it came to him that, in considering staying at Cloona, she was thinking not of herself but of what was best for him.

"No need to be so solemn, lad." His uncle smiled down at Owen. "Come, take a walk with me. I need it after the long ride."

"Had the French ships come sooner, would it have made a difference?" Owen asked, as they stepped outdoors.

"We but awaited them and the guns they carried to break out of the siege. We had despaired of their coming when the English offered terms. Supplies were running so low that the city could not hold out much longer. Well, no use going into all that now. I only hope and pray that your mother will decide to sail for France while there is the opportunity."

That was Owen's fervent hope as he looked at his mother the next morning. He suspected that she had not slept much, for her face was pale and there were shadows under her eyes. She hardly smiled as she greeted him at the breakfast table. Uncle Richard, booted and spurred, with his sword at his side, followed her into the room. He would not stay long after the meal, Owen knew. He looked at his mother expectantly, but she was silent while Anna served them. When Anna had left the room, it was Uncle Richard who spoke.

"Well, Margaret! I cannot wait longer for your answer."

"I know. I wish it would please you. Though I appreciate your generous offer, Richard, I cannot accept it. I shall stay here."

"Mother! You would take the oath of allegiance to the Orangeman!"

"Margaret, have you thought how that will appear when we return to drive the foreigner out?" Richard asked.

"Yes, I have thought of it. But, Richard, I have so little hope. And if the army should return, surely they will not deal harshly with a widow whose husband died in their cause, and whose brother-in-law is an officer of that army."

"Margaret, I feel this is wrong. I have warned you of Hugh, and if I had the power, I would insist on your coming."

"But you haven't. I cannot abandon my son's inheritance nor the people who depend on us."

Owen looked from one to the other. His mother's face was set in firm lines and his uncle appeared too indignant to speak. Through the window, Owen could see Patrick leading Richard's horse towards the avenue.

Richard got to his feet. Owen and his mother rose also. She went to her brother-in-law with outstretched hands.

"Richard, let us not part in anger. You are the only one left to Owen and me. Let us be friends. We shall meet again, here, if you are right. If not, someday in France."

At the door Richard held out his right hand to Margaret. "Of course we shall part friends. You and Owen are always close to my heart. Remember, should danger threaten, go to Bart Flaherty in Limerick. He is a loyal friend and a wise man. One thing more: never allow that hidden grant to fall into Hugh's hands."

"Not while I live."

Richard walked with a firm step to where his horse was waiting. As he mounted and rode away, Owen wondered what hidden grant Uncle Richard had meant.

CHAPTER TWO

When Owen could no longer hear the hoofbeats, he followed his mother into the house, closing the great oak door behind him.

"Let us go into the study," she said. "There is something I must tell you."

Now he would hear the explanation of his uncle's mysterious warning, Owen thought. His mother sat in front of the fire. Owen, too impatient to sit down, stood in front of her, his back to the hearth.

"My son, you are only a boy, but you must take on the responsibilities of a man. For with Richard gone, there is no one else."

A note of appeal in her voice made a shiver run up Owen's spine in spite of the warmth from the fire. His mother, who had always treated him like a child, now looked to him for strength. He moved away from the hearth and sat down opposite her.

Mrs. Bourke leaned back in her chair, looking into the fire, as she continued, "You are wondering what your uncle meant when he spoke of the grant because I have never told you about it. I did not want to burden you, but now you must help me to keep it safe for you."

"But where is it? And what is it? What is this all about?"

"Have a little patience, Owen." His mother spoke in a more familiar tone. "You have often heard your father speak of that William Bourke, your great grandfather's younger brother, who went to Lord Baltimore's Colony of Maryland."

"I remember sitting on Father's knee while he showed me on the map where it was and how far a journey from Cloona."

"You will recall, then, that William Bourke's wife and children died in the wilderness. But you did not know that William left the manor granted to him by Lord Baltimore to your grandfather who, in Cromwell's time, seriously considered taking your grandmother and their children there. Only his fear that the hardships in a new country might be too severe restrained him. The grant of land descended to your father and now it is yours, as long as it remains in your possession. That is the condition under which William Bourke left it to your grandfather and the eldest son of his line."

"Wasn't it strange for a younger son to leave his land that way?"

"Perhaps not as strange as it seems. Then, as now, Catholics might lose their lands in Ireland, as well as in England. He probably wanted to provide a refuge so that the Bourke family might not disappear as so many Irish families have. Your father believed that he made possession of the grant a condition of ownership, in case it became impossible to trace the eldest son and resulted in title reverting to the king. So you can see how important it is to keep it safe and why Hugh might covet it."

"Do you think that's why he came here so often of late? He did not come when Father was living."

"It could be. I wanted to believe it was out of sympathy and family feeling, but a man who is traitor to king and country is hardly capable of such sentiments. If Hugh thought to learn about the grant from me, he failed."

Owen was surprised at the vehemence in his mother's voice.

"But where is the grant, Mother? Is it hidden somewhere in this room?"

"In a way, yes." His mother stood and went to the bookshelves built flush with the fireplace on the side where Owen was sitting. He stood beside her as she removed two books from the end of the third shelf. Taking his hand in hers, she guided it along the notched molding which covered the angle at the back of the shelf. As she moved his hand up, she counted each notch. "One, two, three, four. Now press your finger there."

Owen did and the bookshelves swung inward slowly like a door. He stepped inside, but the light from the room showed only the stone wall of the chimney. His mother had turned to light a candle at the fire. Then she followed him into the hollow space, guarding the flame with her hand. By its wavering light Owen could see the other two walls were of stone also. Against the opposite wall stood a small chest of drawers and at right angles to it a narrow pallet.

When she had placed the candle on the chest, his mother swung the bookcase wall back into position so that Owen could see the heavy cloth lining it to deaden sound. Then she pointed out the bolt which held it fast.

"When it is in place," she explained, "the spring on the other side will not work. Anyone hiding here would be quite safe."

Owen had been too amazed to speak, but now he asked, "How is it that I have never known this place was here? Why was it built?"

"I'll tell you about it later. Come over here now." She turned back to the chest and pulled out the lower drawer. She lifted out a cloth-wrapped bundle and placed it on the top, opening it enough so that Owen could see the priest's vestments within.

"Now, Owen, press against the bottom right hand corner of the drawer."

When Owen did, the other end of the board lifted up. Beneath lay the two yellowed papers of the grant. Owen picked them up to examine the faded writing and the great seals.

"You had better put them back, Owen. We should not linger here."

Owen obeyed reluctantly, and when they were in place, the vestments were returned and the drawer closed. His mother held the candle high so that he could look into the darkness above. "It goes up to the roof," she said, "where there is a hidden vent which lets in air. Come, we will talk about it in the study."

She held the candle so that Owen could push back the bolt and swing the bookshelf wall open.

Seated again before the fire in the study, Owen noticed that the room looked exactly as it had before his mother had revealed its secret.

"I can hardly believe it is really there," Owen said, looking at the familiar bookshelves increduously. "Tell me about it."

"When your grandfather returned from France at the Restoration, he found, as you know, that Cloona had been destroyed by Cromwell's troops. Only a part of the old central chimney still stood. It was huge, as it had served the fireplaces in the large hall on one side and the kitchen on the other. Your grandfather built the new Cloona in the current style, but used the old chimney here, while leaving a space for a priest's hiding place, as was common practice in England. He also stored there altar vessels and vestments, everything needed to celebrate the Mass."

"But when grandfather came back from France, the priests came too, didn't they?" Owen asked.

"Yes they did, in Ireland, but they were still forbidden in England and your grandfather realized that the time might come when they could not go openly here. Meanwhile, the hidden room was the safest place to keep the Maryland grant and it has remained hidden there all these years, but protected from decay by the warmth from the fireplace and fresh air from the vent in the roof."

"And are you the only one who knows about it?"

"Your uncle knows and now you do too. If at any time

we have to leave Cloona, I shall rely on you to see that the documents go with us. As the heir of the Bourkes, they are yours. I need not add that you must speak of this to no one." His mother stood up and went quickly out of the room.

Owen sighed as he got up and walked over to the long window that overlooked the garden. He thought of his uncle far on the road to Limerick. Soon he would be gone over the sea, and left in Ireland would be Cousin Hugh in the English camp.

Seeing Brian in the lane near the stables, Owen opened the window and stepped out. The dog came running towards him. Owen threw a stick and as Brian ran to retrieve it, Owen ran after him, fresh air and movement dispersing the gloom which had hung around him. A manor in Lord Baltimore's Colony! A better inheritance than the dwindling acres of Cloona! He would go and claim it someday, he decided, as the stick was retrieved. He walked with Brian towards the stables. There he found Patrick cleaning out stalls as he grumbled to himself.

"What's the matter?" Owen called out.

Patrick came limping towards him. "I don't like Mr. Richard going off to France and leaving you and your mother here alone," he answered, his furrowed brow indicating the troubled state of his mind. "I don't like it at all. Now if I had two good legs under me, I wouldn't be so worried, but I'm not the man I used to be."

"You're all the man we need," Owen assured him.

"That I'm not, Master Owen. I'm afraid Mr. Richard's

right and that false-hearted Hugh Bourke'll bring trouble."

He stood in the doorway, gazing up at the clouds hanging low over the roof, as if they menaced the safety of the woman and boy he was bound to protect. Finally he broke the silence, "Master Owen, there is something I must do that I do not want to do. It's the only thing, the only thing," he repeated, as if to reassure himself.

"Well, what is it? Can I help you with it?"

"You must help me. Come with me where I can be sure there are no listening ears."

This seemed unnecessary to Owen, for he could see young Gavin Dooley, the stable boy, over by the kitchen door, and he was the only other person who came to the stables. Owen, however, followed Patrick around the house and down the avenue to the gate. Patrick leaned against the stone pillar, while Owen threw the stick which Brian raced to recover.

"Let the dog be," Patrick said as Brian stood waiting for the stick to be thrown again. "You remember Bart Flaherty?"

"How could I forget him? His house in Irishtown is the last place I went with my father before he and you rode off to the war."

"A sad memory, lad, but I'm glad you recall it, for you may need to know it one of these days. There's one other place you should know. I'll be taking you there myself this afternoon. You're to tell no one, not even your mother. That's the part I don't like about it." Patrick sighed. "It's not in my heart to have you deceive her, but there's no other way."

"Where is this place and what is its secret?" Owen wondered how many hiding places he had missed in the years he had been playing around Cloona.

"Let be, lad. I'll tell you no more. This is what you must do. I'll have Sheelah saddled for you this afternoon, instead of Donegal. You'll ride to that knot of beech trees over beyond the village on the Ennis road. You know the place?"

"Yes, of course."

"I'll meet you there one hour after the midday meal is over. Should anyone ask your errand, you're taking some horse medicine to Tom Hogan for me. I'll have it tied to the saddle."

"Where are we going from there?" Owen asked, impatient with all the mystery.

"We'll talk no more about it. Just be there as I said. Now back to your books. Remember, not a word to anyone."

Owen went, seething at being treated one moment as if he were a man and the next ordered back to his studies as if he were still a child.

In the afternoon he went to the stables as Patrick had directed. There he found Sheelah saddled and bridled, even the medicine bottle tied to the saddle. Donegal was restless in his stall and Owen stroked the hunter's nose. "Patrick would have saddled you if it were safe, but you know I can't take you on the high road."

Owen turned away to mount the little Irish pony.

There was no one on the road as Sheelah trotted towards the village. Owen thought of his uncle, whom he would not see for many months. If only they could have talked about the Maryland grant. Maybe someday they would go together to claim the Bourke inheritance.

Near the village there was a gap in the hedgerow through which Cloona could be seen across the fields. When he came to it, Owen halted his horse. This view had always pleased him, but today the gray stone house in the gray fields under the dull sky looked dreary enough. But it was home. He hated to think of it falling into Hugh's hands, though he might not be able to prevent it. But the Maryland acres Hugh would not get.

As he rode through the village, Owen noticed how many roofs needed thatching against the winter rains. Unless some of the men now with the army came home, Owen did not know how the thatching was going to be accomplished. Many of them would probably sail to France, taking their families with them, and there would be no one to care if the rain came in.

At their meeting place, Patrick was waiting, seated on a horse Owen had never seen before. With its shaggy coat and long fetlocks, it looked as if it might belong to the rapparees, who did not groom their mounts as Patrick did Sheelah.

"Did you meet any on the road?" Patrick asked as he swung his horse in beside Sheelah.

"Not a one."

"That's good."

The short reply was so unlike Patrick that Owen stared at him. A grimace of pain passed over Patrick's face as the horses broke into a run. Indeed Patrick was not the man he used to be, Owen realized. He would ask no more questions, though he was full of curiosity about their destination.

When they had gone about a mile, Patrick pointed to a track across the bog. "There's our road," he said, turning his horse's head. "We must travel single file here. See the wooded hill that rises over to the right?"

Owen nodded, looking across the undulating bogland to where, about a quarter of a mile away, a clump of trees rose, and beyond it other hills reached toward the sky.

Patrick held his horse in check as he turned his head from left to right to make sure that no one was in sight.

"The hiding place of the rapparees is in that first clump of trees. It is known only to them and to me. I'm taking you there, for I fear the time may come when we shall need their protection and," with a wry glance at his knee, "I might not be able to get here in time.'Tis a heavy secret I'm confiding in you, lad. Swift and terrible will be the punishment if you betray it."

Owen's heart was beating fast as he followed Patrick. He had heard many times of these lawless bands, but he had never expected to be brought to their lair. His mother would not sanction this visit. Yet nowhere else would there be protection for her if help were needed.

Watching the track carefully as it wound through the bog, Owen soon realized that the surefooted Sheelah would find it better than he if they came this way again.

They reached the trees that marked the end of the bog. Within their shade Patrick stopped his horse, but remained motionless in the saddle. Abruptly a man stood before them. He seemed to have sprung from the earth. He wore the long frieze coat and tight trousers of a peasant, but his swarthy skin and long black hair marked him as different from the men who had tilled the fields around Cloona. He came close to Patrick and spoke in a voice so low that Owen could not hear what he said.

Then Patrick dismounted and motioned Owen to do the same. The black-haired man took the reins of their horses while Patrick started forward on foot. Owen followed, watching his steps carefully on the hummocky land where roots and fallen branches reached out to trip him. The ascent was steep and Patrick went slowly. After climbing for several minutes, he came to a halt before a large boulder which stood up like a miniature cliff among the trees. He rested a moment there, then walked beside the boulder to its end. When he vanished from Owen's sight, the boy was frightened. What sort of a place was this where men appeared and disappeared without warning. He had heard that the rapparees could melt into the air, when pursued, but he had never known Patrick to do so before. Having no choice, Owen followed the path skirting the rock until he came to the narrow entrance to a cave. It seemed that Patrick had gone in, so Owen stepped forward into inky blackness.

"Take my hand, lad." Patrick's whispered words were welcome. Together they took a few steps forward, then making a sharp turn, entered a larger cave. On a table in the center a fat tallow candle cast wavering shadows over the damp walls and illuminated the face of the man who sat facing them, his dark brows frowning over deep-set eyes. Although he wore the gray frieze of a peasant, his shirt was fine linen.

"Who is this you have brought here, Patrick?" he asked.

"You know well, Murrough O'Cahane, that it is Owen Bourke."

A brief smile eased the frown from O'Cahane's face.

"Welcome, Master Owen. I knew your grandfather well. He strove to have my lands restored when King Charles returned to England, but in vain. Though my father's blood was shed for the king in Flanders, he cared little about the widow and orphaned children. And now the Bourkes are like to lose their lands, too."

"I hope not, sir. My mother has elected to remain in Ireland to hold them, if such be the will of God."

"The will of our English masters rather," O'Cahane said fiercely. "Think you they will consult the will of God, or right or justice, when they see good lands in the hands of an Irishman?"

"But under the treaty our possession is confirmed," Owen argued.

"And will William keep that treaty with those who fought for the Stuarts, when neither Charles nor James kept their word to the men who risked life and fortune for them?"

Owen was silenced.

"But that is not what you came here today to discuss," O'Cahane went on in a milder tone. "Patrick tells me that your mother has only him and you to protect her should your fair cousin Hugh decide to seize your land."

"Should that happen, we must go to my Uncle Richard in France."

"Unless you care to join my band," O'Cahane count-

36

ered. "There are lads no older than you in it. There is plenty of excitement and many a wrong to be righted, which else would never be righted." He looked intently at Owen, who returned the gaze proudly.

"I cannot join, sir. My mother would never consent and I must stay with her, for she has no one else."

"Well spoken, lad. When the time comes that you need the help of the rapparees, it will be given. Now, there is one here I want you to know." A smile lighted his face at an exclamation from Patrick. "I know this is unusual, but young Sean may serve us better if he and Owen know each other. He is one of my band who is about your age," he explained to Owen.

The rapparee leader got out of his chair and walked towards the entrance of the cave. In a moment the rock walls resounded with the sharp whistle of a curlew's call. Owen jumped at the sound, turning quickly as if he expected to see one of the seabirds behind him. Patrick grinned at Owen's surprise but said nothing as O'Cahane returned, followed by a tall youth whose brown hair framed a face so thin that the bones stood out sharply.

"Owen, this is Sean O'Kelly. Should we need to send a message direct to you, Sean will bring it. When he does, you'll do exactly as he says."

Having looked Owen over from head to foot, Sean said, "I'll know him again."

"Then be off with you." At O'Cahane's command, Sean went quickly from the cave.

"Patrick, have you taught Owen the signal?"

"That I haven't and wouldn't until you gave the word."

"Come then." O'Cahane led the way out of the cave. Standing well within the shadow of its guardian rock, he twice whistled the long high note of the curlew, then after an interval twice again. From below came the answering call twice, a pause, then three times.

"You hear how it goes, lad." O'Cahane put his hand on Owen's shoulder. "Should it be necessary for you to come here, you must stop as soon as you are under the trees and give that signal. Wait for the reply. Either you will hear the answering whistle from this cave or some-one will meet you there. Come only if you need us. Our life does not permit casual visitors."

Thus dismissed, Owen followed Patrick to the place where their horses waited. As a quiet word passed be-tween the guard and Patrick, Owen was aware that the man was observing him carefully. Then after mounting, Owen and Patrick rode away. A chill wind blew from the west, bringing gray mist to settle on the bog. It gave an eerie quality to the late afternoon, though Owen was no stranger to the bog and the mist.

CHAPTER THREE

One January morning when Owen came to the breakfast table, there was a small leather box at his place.

"What's this?" he asked his mother who was pouring
tea from the silver pot.

"Open it and see."

Owen lifted the lid and saw his father's watch lying on
the faded velvet lining. He took it out, asking, "Why are
you giving it to me today?"

"Richard brought it to me after your father's death.
We both felt it should be yours. Your father treasured it.
He would want you to have it, for you are the man of the
family now."

Owen wound the stem. He could almost feel his
father's strong gentle hand over his, at the familiar gesture.

"Thank you, Mother." He could not keep the tremor
out of his voice.

Owen placed the watch carefully in the pocket of his

waistcoat. He was conscious of its light pressure all morning as he worked at Latin and French.

At dinner his mother returned to the subject most on her mind, though Owen had long ago wearied of it. "We must plan now for the spring, Owen. It will be upon us before we know it."

"But how?" Only the slight pressure of the watch against his ribs kept the impatience out of his voice. "There's only Tim Lafflin and John Sheehy returned of the twenty men who went to the war and the two of them are not equal to one; John with his right arm gone and Tim with a bullet through his ankle."

"I know, but there are boys enough to tend some sheep, and Tim can still guide a plough."

"And where's the money to come from to buy the sheep?" This time Owen failed to keep the sharpness out of his tone.

"We could have the wood cut down and sold," his mother suggested.

"Cut down the wood? Don't you remember how angry Father was with Uncle Richard when he suggested that?"

"I do, indeed, but we must be practical. If we are to keep Cloona, something must be done. We could cut only the further part, leaving a grove directly behind the house. Then we would not miss the rest."

Owen considered the idea, but before he was ready to reply, he heard the sound of a horse's hoofs on the avenue. He looked inquiringly at his mother, for seldom in these days did anyone come to Cloona. Owen rose to answer the knock at the door, his mother following him into the hall.

When Owen swung open the door, a soldier in the uniform of King William's grenadiers stepped in. Looking from mother to son, he said, "I have a communication for Mistress Margaret Bourke."

"I am Mistress Bourke," she said, stepping forward. She held out her hand into which the soldier put a sealed paper.

Patrick, who had come from the stable, took charge of horse and rider while Owen closed the door and went with his mother to the study.

Seated before the fire, Mrs. Bourke broke the seal and read the contents quickly. Then she handed the document to Owen, without a word. Struggling through the unfamiliar legal terms, he made out that the King's Court had named Hugh Bourke guardian of his cousin Owen, son of James and Margaret Bourke, on condition that the boy be brought up in the Protestant religion. As guardian, Hugh would control, during Owen's minority, Cloona and any other estates in Ireland of which James Bourke had died possessed.

Owen's impulse was to toss the offending document into the fire, but he realized in time that such a gesture would accomplish nothing.

"We need not worry about cutting down the wood," he said, his voice louder than he intended. "Hugh will see to it and to all else that has troubled you, with little care for my father's wishes or the needs of our people."

"I had not believed that Hugh would do this to me."

His mother's face was pale and her eyes were dark with pain. "If only Richard were still here."

"Hugh wouldn't have dared while Uncle Richard was in the country. But there must be something we can do—someone who can help us." Owen thought of O'Cahane but could not mention that name to his mother.

"I must send to your father's friend Bart Flaherty for advice." His mother spoke in her calm, firm way, having overcome the momentary weakness caused by the unexpected blow. "Will you see if the soldier has gone? Better not go through the kitchen where Ellie and Anna will want to know what's going on."

Relieved to have something to do, Owen went to the long window leading to the garden. He opened it, stepped out, and walked quickly along the path which led to the stables. He came to the break in the hedge in time to see the soldier come from the kitchen and mount the horse which Patrick held. As soon as horse and rider had gone around the corner of the house, Owen called Patrick, who came as quickly as he could.

"Mother wants to see you," Owen said, leading the way back to the study.

When Patrick stood before her, Mrs. Bourke told him what the document contained, for Patrick could not read the English words.

"The blackguard!" he exclaimed as he examined the official seals. "I knew he'd do something, but couldn't guess at such villiany."

"Patrick, I must know if this is final and what I should do. Richard told me to send to Bart Flaherty if I needed advice, and I need it now."

"Yes, madam. He's the man to consult. I doubt he'd come here, but if you'll trust me to send it to him, I think I'll have an answer quickly."

"Take it, Patrick. I am most anxious for his opinion as soon as possible. I'll write a note to go with it."

When the note was written, Patrick took it and the notice from the King's Court and left. When he had gone, Owen paced nervously around the room, while his mother sat looking blankly into the fire. There seemed nothing to do, nothing at all, but to wait.

At last his mother spoke. "Owen, we must be prepared for whatever comes. I fear this means that Cloona is lost. I think that Hugh may come soon, and we must not be here if he does. Once he is in control, there would be nothing we could do."

"Mother!" Owen was facing the bookshelves. "Did you notice there was no mention of the Maryland manor? Why do you suppose it was not included? Is it possible that Hugh does not know of it?"

"I'm sure he does. Most likely he is also aware that possession of the deed would allow him to claim it with no further provisions. As long as we hold it, that he cannot do. It would be well to get it now. Everything of value that we can take should be in one place." She stood up, but she was trembling so, she had to grasp the back of the chair for support. Owen went quickly to her side, placing his arm around her. "What is it, Mother? Are you ill?"

"No." She leaned against him. "It's too much—too sudden —"

"Perhaps you'd better lie down—"

"No, Owen." The trembling ceased as if by an effort of her will. "Help me to my room." His arm still around her, Owen went with her through the hall and up the stairs. When they came to her room, he helped her onto the bed, then stood looking down at her, not knowing what to do.

"Do not worry, Owen." His mother's voice was under control. "I'll be over this in a minute. Send Anna to me. I'll leave it to you to get the documents."

Owen hurried from the room and, taking the stairs two at a time, ran to the kitchen, where he was sure to find Anna. When the maid left to go to her mistress, Ellie looked at him curiously.

"Such comings and goings. Your mother must have Anna right away and Patrick says 'If you see Master Owen, send him to me in the stable.' And what it's all about I wouldn't know."

Owen scarcely heard the last words. He was already out the door. He should have known that Patrick would want him to ride to the cave.

Patrick was in the stable yard with Sheelah saddled and bridled. "'Twill be quicker than summoning the rapparees here, and likely O'Cahane will want to see you. Here's the documents to be sent to Bart Flaherty. Go quickly, but be careful that no one sees you when you take the track through the bog. I'll explain to your mother. She'll have to know now."

Owen rode off down the avenue and along the road towards the village at a fast pace until he came to the gap in the hedge through which he could see Cloona. He halted Sheelah and looked over at the gray house with the dark woods behind it. Only an hour ago his mother had talked about selling those woods. Now it would be Hugh who would do it, with no sentiment to deter him. There must be some way to prevent him from taking possession. Owen gave Sheelah a slap to start her running again.

Before he came to the village, he had to turn his horse aside, for ahead of him on the road were a woman with a baby in her arms and three small children stumbling wearily along beside her. When he came up to her, Owen drew rein long enough to assure her that there was shelter in the village beyond where no one was so poor that he had not a bit of food and a roof to share with these wanderers of the road.

Owen did not need to ask their story. Ever since the Irish foot soldiers had embarked at Cork, where their families were turned back from the ships on which they too had been promised passage, such little family groups had been traveling the Irish roads. These women and children, with no man to provide for them, were stumbling back to a home which now offered no more than shelter against the bitter winter winds. Many times his mother had sent clothing for those who sought temporary refuge in the village. Who would care for them when she was gone, when she and her son were refugees, too, Owen asked bitterly, urging Sheelah into a gallop.

Absorbed in his angry thoughts, he was almost at the place where the track left the road when he remembered Patrick's warning. He would have to take time to ride beyond, time that he should not have used, he thought as he gradually slowed Sheelah's pace and at a safe distance turned back. Scanning the road carefully as he came to the track, he was relieved to see no one. He wheeled Sheelah to the left across the bog towards the hill which hid the rapparee's cave.

When he came to the end of the track, he drew rein. After waiting a moment under the silent trees, he whistled twice, paused, then twice again. He watched carefully, determined that this time he would not be surprised by one of O'Cahane's men. Then from the direction of the cave he heard the answering call, twice, a pause, then three times. After jumping down, he tied Sheelah's reins to a branch of a tree and walked towards the cave. How still it was! Had it not been for the answering signal, he would have thought no one was near.

At the entrance to the cave he almost stumbled against the man standing there. After a silent scrutiny the guard moved aside and motioned Owen to enter. Stepping into the darkness, Owen tried to recall how many steps there were before the turn. He could not remember, so he moved cautiously, one hand touching the wall beside him, the other arm stretched out in front. After ten steps, which he had carefully counted this time, his extended hand touched rock. Then turning, he could see the wavering light from the candle. O'Cahane sat at the table as before. The scene was so exactly as Owen remembered, that it was strange not to have Patrick beside him.

Stepping into the circle of light, Owen waited until O'Cahane lifted his head.

"So, Master Owen, you have come to claim the help I promised you."

"Yes, sir." Owen held out the court order and his

mother's note to O'Cahane. "Patrick asks that you send these to Bart Flaherty in Limerick immediately, but first I would like you to read them, so you will know our danger."

O'Cahane glanced through the opened parchment, his lips held in a thin straight line, his black brows drawn together in a scowl. When he had finished, he tossed it on the table.

"I fear there is nothing Bart or anyone can do. The King's Court has made Hugh your guardian, and there is little likelihood of an appeal by your mother prevailing against him. However, the message will be sent. Meanwhile, you should be ready to leave at any moment, unless you intend to remain and become Hugh Bourke's ward." He raised an inquiring eyebrow.

Owen's face flamed. "Never, sir. My mother is already preparing to leave."

"Good! And where will you go?"

"Where else but to France and my Uncle Richard?"

"Aye, where else?" O'Cahane echoed. "And this will happen again and again throughout the length and breadth of the land, till not a rightful owner is left in possession of his home, unless he abjure his ancient faith and his loyal friends. God help the poor people who are left when you and all like you have fled to other lands, Owen Bourke."

Owen looked in the burning brown eyes. "What else would you have us do, sir?"

"I know well there is nothing else you can do, lad. But I mourn for this poor land of ours, robbed of its best blood and left with only the peasants to be ground underfoot by Hugh Bourke and his like. But we must make plans. You say your mother is making preparations to leave. Tell her she can take little with her. When the time comes, you will have no coach or packhorses. Have ready only what can be carried in saddlebags. There will be just you and your mother?"

"There is Anna who came with mother. She has no one here. We could not leave her. And Patrick—"

"Patrick stays here," O'Cahane broke in.

"Patrick will not want to remain without—"

"Patrick is needed here. He will stay. So, you will want to have three horses. You have the garron you rode over. I will provide two more."

"We have Donegal," Owen pointed out. "We will need only one other."

"Donegal, like Patrick, remains. Do not worry. Hugh shall not have him. But there are too few such horses left in Ireland. You would be easy to trace, if you rode him. Patrick and I will see to Donegal. After all, you could hardly manage to get him to France with you."

"Of course you're right. And maybe I'll come back to claim him some day with the army."

At this remark, O'Cahane smiled but made no comment. His next words were spoken like a command, "You will need peasants' clothing for travel. Tell your mother to see to it. Have all that you intend taking ready to pick up at a moment's notice. I shall know if Hugh Bourke is coming. You must be ready to leave immediately, when I send word, not even waiting to hear from Bart Flaherty. It may be tonight. Now go."

Owen left the cave and walked slowly down the hill to

where Sheelah was tethered. He untied and mounted her, and then turned into the track across the bog. The warning echoed in his ears "... be ready to leave immediately ... it may be tonight."

CHAPTER FOUR

Back at Cloona, Owen led Sheelah into the stable, O'Cahane's words still ringing in his ears. Was this to be the last time he would unsaddle Sheelah, he thought, leading her into the stall and loosening the girth. He could not believe that his home was to pass into the possession of his cousin Hugh, while, disguised as peasants, he and his mother were to make their way to France.

Sheelah safely tethered, Owen stopped to pat Donegal's nose. Leaving home would not be so bitter if he could ride away still in the habit of a gentleman, on this horse. Donegal nickered softly and Owen rested his cheek against the horse's firm neck, as he whispered good-bye.

Leaving the stable, he walked quickly toward the study, avoiding the kitchen, from which came the sound and smell of a meal being prepared. He did not want to talk to anyone, least of all Ellie, her curiosity still unsatisfied. As he latched the window behind him, he stood for a moment, thinking he should light a candle and get the papers from their hiding place now. Remembering how he had left his mother, he felt he must go to her immediately. How would she take the instructions he brought from O'Cahane, he wondered, as he crossed the study and went into the hall. How could she possibly be ready to leave tonight, if they had to? He ran up the stairs to her room. To his astonishment he found her standing by her bed composedly sorting clothes.

"Mother!"

She turned, smiling at the exclamation. "I'm all right now, Owen. It was but a momentary weakness. What did the rapparee leader say?"

"That we must be ready to go at a moment's notice. We can take with us only what can be packed in saddlebags."

"That is what I anticipated. Anna and I have been getting together what we will most need, if we must go."

"There's little doubt of that. O'Cahane says that we must be dressed as peasants."

"Yes. It is fortunate that I had been collecting warm clothing for the poor families who come this way. You will find a suit of frieze in your room. Anna and I have gowns and cloaks in readiness."

Anna came bustling into the room. "I've made a pocket in Master Owen's coat, ma'am, as you bade me," she said. "It is stoutly sewn. That frieze is good, strong cloth, though rough. He could carry a pound of gold in it without fear of it giving away. What would you want me to do next?"

"You might find Patrick and have him bring in the

51

saddlebags. It would be well to have everything in readiness when the summons comes."

"And it could come tonight." The harsh tone, as much as Owen's words, startled his mother. She dropped the shirt she had been folding. "So soon! I had thought—" Breaking off, she turned to Anna, standing trembling in the doorway.

"Please go find Patrick, as I asked."

"Yes, ma'am." Anna went towards the stairs, her sighs audible in the room.

"Owen, it was unnecessary to alarm Anna that way."

His mother's chiding heightened Owen's irritation to anger. "How can you accept all this so calmly, Mother? My blood boils at the thought of Hugh here, enjoying all that my father died defending so that it might one day be mine."

"Your father died for more than that, Owen. He fought to preserve for Ireland its ancient faith and rightful king. Always remember that for him the faith came first. If we must leave Cloona to keep it, we are doing his will. You would not do otherwise, Owen?" She looked questioningly at her son.

"Of course not, Mother," Owen managed the few words in his normal voice, but inwardly he still seethed with anger.

"That is well. Now, to more practical things." His mother picked up a small leather bag from the chest of drawers. "This contains my jewels and most of the gold coins we possess. I shall conceal it under my gown." She put the bag back on the chest, taking up a small purse which she held out to Owen. "There is enough gold in this to see you safely to France, if we should be separated. Guard it well."

Owen took it from her hand silently. He was still too angry to speak, without risking another rebuke from his mother.

"I think it would be wise, Owen, if you went to your room and put on the frieze suit, to be sure it is all right. You will find the pocket in the hem which Anna has prepared to conceal the Maryland grant. When you are ready, come and let me see you. Meanwhile, Anna and I will get the saddlebags packed, and all will be in readiness if we should have to leave tonight."

Obediently Owen went to his room. At the sight of the frieze suit lying on his bed, his anger flared again. Having taken off his broadcloth breeches, which though worn were still the habit of a gentleman, he pulled on the long, tight trousers, the coarse stuff scratching his legs. With a grimace he exchanged his fine linen shirt for the coarse homespun one and put on the long coat which hung below his knees. He found the opening which Anna had made in the hem and dropped in the purse and his father's watch.

Standing before a long mirror, he was astounded to see how well he would pass for a peasant. Opening his mouth, he let his jaw hang down and the transformation was complete. But he would not, like a peasant, passively accept the inevitable, he vowed. Before he would leave Cloona for Hugh, he would burn it to the ground. And why not, he thought. A lighted stick applied to the staircase, a few burning twigs igniting the drawing room draperies and within half an hour the blaze would spread through the house. He went back to his mother's room. Her look of pained surprise confirmed his own unhappy conviction that he resembled too well the peasant whose clothes he wore. She said, "The coat is too long, but we will not worry about that. You have found the opening Anna made, so that you can carry the documents in the hem?"

"Yes, Mother." Owen patted the left side of the coat. "The purse you gave me is already there. I'll go now to get the documents."

"You're sure you can manage it alone?" She broke off as Anna came to the door, dragging the saddlebags. "Fine, Anna. Let us see if the bags will hold the clothing I have collected. Owen, call me if you need my help."

Thus dismissed, Owen hurried through the upper hall and down the stairs. A peat fire was burning in the fireplace in the lower hall. If there was kindling in the cupboard beside it, all would be ready when the moment came. Owen opened its door only to find that Gavin had neglected to fill it. Owen knew he could get some wood from the shed by the kitchen. Going quickly through the hall and the study, he opened the long window and stepped into the garden. When he came to the gap in the hedge, he heard a horse's hooves on the cobblestones of the yard and drew back into the shadows as the rider alighted and went into Patrick's cabin.

There was no time to lose. Owen raced across the dusky yard to the shed, gathered an armful of dry branches, and ran back to the safety of the hedge. He reached it as the door of Patrick's cabin opened. Owen darted back to the study, taking a moment to secure the window, then into the hall. As he put the wood in the cupboard, he heard footsteps on the stone floor of the passageway from the kitchen. He only had time to brush into the fireplace the dry leaves which had clung to his coat, when the door opened and O'Cahane entered, followed by Patrick.

"Well, Master Owen!" There was a gleam in the rapparee's eyes. "Pull a lock of hair over your forehead and you'll pass for a peasant lad anywhere."

Since this drew only an angry look from Owen, O'Cahane's face resumed its normally stern expression. "Where's your mother, lad? The time has come sooner even than I thought."

Mrs. Bourke appeared at the head of the stairs. Seeing the stranger with Patrick, she came down in her quick, graceful way. He might never see her on that stairway again, Owen thought.

With a bow which proclaimed him no untutored peasant, O'Cahane spoke: "I regret that I bring bad news, madam. You must leave Cloona at once. Word has come from Limerick that Hugh is preparing to ride here tonight. He had not intended you to know of the guardianship until he came, and now, in anger, hastens here."

Owen saw his mother's face pale, but she answered O'Cahane with perfect composure. "Anna and I will change immediately. Since Owen is already dressed for the journey, perhaps he could have some supper while we do so."

"A good idea, madam. I'll tell your cook to bring it in and to prepare bread and meat for you to take with you, as no time must be lost." Bowing, O'Cahane left them.

"You may bring the saddlebags down, if you will, Patrick." Mrs. Bourke went towards the stairs and Owen walked into the dining room, where the table had already been laid. The candlelight was reflected back from silver and china and polished wood. The tapestried walls were dark in the corners. The contrast between his rough clothing and the richly appointed room rekindled his anger. Hugh would not sit here at his ease, Owen vowed. Somehow when the others left he would manage to stay in the house to set it on fire. Meanwhile, as soon as Patrick went out with the saddlebags, the precious papers must be taken from their hiding place.

Ellie entered with a steaming bowl of broth. "Now sit you down, Master Owen, and eat this up. It will give you strength for your sad journey. If I were younger, you'd not be leaving me behind to wait on that blackguard Hugh. If he thinks I'll cook meals for him that are fit to eat, he's mistaken. With your mother gone, I'll not be able to remember the skill she taught me, that I won't."

Owen had sat down while she talked, and he took a spoonful of broth, hoping to hurry her from the room. But she continued to stand over him. "Now eat it all, Master Owen. It may be a long time before you eat again."

"Ellie," he asked in desperation. "have you got the meat and bread ready for us?"

" 'Twill be the work of a moment." As she went out of the room, Patrick came down the stairs dragging two saddlebags. Owen went into the hall to help him, hoping thus to gain a few minutes in which to get the documents. As he did, O'Cahane came through the door from the kitchen passage and Mrs. Bourke appeared at the head of the stairs.

"Are you ready?" O'Cahane asked, taking one of the bags from Patrick, as Owen grasped the other. Anna was bumping the third bag down the stairs behind Mrs. Bourke. She said to Owen, as she reached the bottom step, "Here's a cloak to wrap around you," and to O'Cahane, "I believe we have everything."

He started through the kitchen passage, followed by Patrick, who had taken the third bag from Anna, when Owen exclaimed, "My watch! I left it in my room."

"It was his father's," Mrs. Bourke explained to O'Cahane, who had turned as if to forbid any delay. "I would hate it to fall into Hugh's hands."

"Very well," O'Cahane answered. "Give me that bag and be quick about it lad. If you, madam, and the maid will come with me, we'll get you onto your horses and the saddlebags attached while we wait."

Owen started up the stairs, but as soon as Patrick had closed the passage door, he leaped back to the hall, opened the cupboard door, and pulled out the bundle of dry branches. After dragging it over to the stair rail, he took a lighted candle from the mantle and held it to the dried leaves. In a moment he had a pinpoint of fire started. One more and he would go to the study. There was no time to get to the drawing room, too.

"You young fool!" One hand grasped his shoulder. The other jerked the candle from his hand. "Step on that flame." It was O'Cahane's voice in a tone Owen dared not disobey. Together they trampled out the blaze. Then the man tossed the smouldering twigs into the hearth where they would do no harm. In their bright flame, he turned to Owen. "What would you do? Light a torch to bring Hugh and his escort here at a gallop? We have little enough time as it is."

"But I will not leave Cloona to him," Owen shouted angrily. "He shall not have it."

"Do you want him to have you, too? If you do not come at once, you will be left."

"But I must get . . ."

"Nothing!" Seizing Owen, O'Cahane flung the boy over his shoulder, as if he were a bag of meal. Owen's head was held firmly against O'Cahane's chest, so that he could not cry out. He could hardly breathe. He squirmed and kicked to no avail.

At the kitchen door O'Cahane set Owen down, but kept a firm grip on his arm. Owen tried to pull away, but O'Cahane's hold was too powerful.

"Please," Owen begged, "I've got to get . . ."

"You must ride at once. Now, will you walk to your horse, or must I carry you?"

"I'll walk." Owen could not bear to have his mother and the others see him carried to where they waited.

O'Cahane stood beside Owen until he had mounted Sheelah. "Join your mother and the maid," he commanded. "They but wait for you. Do not speak until you get to the ford. Not a word!" Turning away, he mounted Donegal.

Patrick handed Sheelah's reins to Owen. Then he grasped the boy's free hand in a silent farewell. As if at a signal, the rapparee by the stable started off, Mrs. Bourke, then Anna following. Owen rode behind them, not daring even to look around as the four horses in single file took the path into the woods. Their hooves made no sound on the soft earth. The trees were silent in the still air. Listening intently, Owen could hear no sound from the stable yard. Had O'Cahane ridden off on Donegal already, he wondered, or was he waiting until they were farther away.

The path they were following would bring them onto the road near Killaloe. It seemed to Owen that at the pace they were going, they would not reach the road until daylight. When at last they came to it, the rapparee drew rein and motioned the others to come up to him. When they were all bunched together, he said in a low voice, "Yonder is the ford. The water is low. The horses will cross easily. On the other side, we take the Limerick road."

He started off, tossing his head so that the hood which had shadowed his face fell back. Owen recognized the thin features of Sean O'Kelly. So it was to this boy scarcely older than himself that O'Cahane had entrusted them. Were they of so little importance, Owen thought angrily.

But his mother and Anna were following Sean. Owen rode after them. When they came to the river's edge, Sean turned to Owen: "You have forded the river before?"

"Many times."

"Then go first, your mother and the maid next, and I will come last."

Sheelah responded willingly to Owen's rein and plunged into the cold water. Drawing his legs up, Owen tried to keep his feet above the water, but he soon felt it seeping through his thick brogans. As the water receded, he looked around to see how the others were faring. His mother was not far behind him, her cloak drawn up around her waist. Sean rode beside Anna, holding her horse's reins while she clung to the pommel of her saddle. The poor thing is probably frightened to death, Owen thought, as Sheelah gained the river's bank, shaking herself vigorously and showering Owen and his mother who had come up beside him.

He looked at her as she wiped her face. "Are you all right, Mother? I'm afraid you'll be ill from riding in those damp clothes."

"Don't worry about me, Owen. I kept my cloak dry and will wrap it around me to keep out the chill. I am concerned about Anna."

Tears were running down the maid's face as she rode up with Sean. Her voice quavered. "I can't go on, ma'am. You'll have to leave me here. I'm worn out."

Mrs. Bourke laid her hand reassuringly on Anna's. "You know I'd never do that, my dear. Take heart and all will be well. The worst is over, isn't it?" She looked to Sean for confirmation. He bowed his head, then said, "But we must not delay. Follow me."

He urged his horse into a fast walk and the others followed, Owen bringing up the rear. Even though the ban on talking was removed at the ford, Owen was glad that there was no opportunity to tell his mother that he did not have the Maryland deed. She would have to know, but he dreaded the revelation. Even more he hated to have to relate his childish attempt to burn Cloona. His cheeks burned with shame at the recollection. How could she ever have any confidence in him again.

They rode on until darkness began to ebb from the sky. Owen knew they must be nearing Limerick, but mist shrouded the land so that nothing was visible beyond the two horses directly ahead of him. At last Sean turned off the highway and, when they had followed him, stopped his horse.

"This path will take us to the cottage where we will leave the horses. Then we will go on foot to Flaherty's."

Owen knew his mother and Anna must be exhausted after long hours in the saddle. They could not walk far. Perhaps they could rest at the cottage, he thought, as the horses walked single file along the narrow track. The slow pace irked Owen. With the growing light, their danger increased. He had no doubt that O'Cahane's men had guarded the way during the night, but it was unlikely that he would risk their presence near the city after dawn. Owen hoped that Sean knew what he was doing.

They came at last to a thatched-roofed cottage hidden among the trees. No smoke rose from the chimney, no dog barked at their approach. Halting his horse, Sean gave the curlew's call. Immediately a man stood at his horse's head.

When he had dismounted, Sean conferred with the rapparee in low tones, then the two of them came over to the waiting three.

"You must get down now," Sean said, extending a hand to Mrs. Bourke, as the other man lifted Anna from the saddle.

Owen jumped down, asking, "Would it be possible for

my mother and Anna to rest at the cottage before going on?"

But his mother said quickly, "That will not be necessary. I prefer to keep on until we arrive at Bart Flaherty's."

"It would be foolhardy to do otherwise," Sean replied. "The sun is already up. Let us go on." He started off along a narrow path which led through marshy land, uneven and hummocky. The other rapparee, still supporting the drooping Anna, gestured to Mrs. Bourke and Owen to follow. Owen took his mother's arm, but unlike Anna, she needed little help. In a few minutes they could see the high gray wall of the city ahead. Owen could not imagine how they were to scale it. When they came close under it, Sean gave the rapparee signal and an answering whistle seemed to come from the top of the wall. Then a basket on a rope descended to their feet.

Sean said to Mrs. Bourke, "You will please to get in madam. You will be taken up first. The maid and your son will follow."

Owen moved forward to help his mother as she stepped calmly into the basket. Seating herself, with her knees touching her chin, she grasped the basket firmly. Owen noticed the glance of approval that passed between Sean and the rapparee as the basket began to rise, swaying and bumping against the rough wall. Then it disappeared, drawn inside an aperture high in the masonry. In a moment it came down empty and Anna, trembling and sobbing, got in. When Owen's turn came, his fingers were scraped by the stone as the basket bumped against the wall. He looked down once to see

Sean standing motionless and alert. The other rapparee had disappeared.

Then the basket was pulled in and rested on the floor of a small room in the wall. A bearded man, with one hand still on the rope, helped Owen to his feet. Owen saw his mother and Anna seated on a bench. He crossed over to them and took his mother's hand. The basket was pushed out the window and in another minute Sean was in the room, grinning at Owen.

The two rapparees then murmured together in that unintelligible way that Owen found exasperating. When they finished, the bearded one addressed Mrs. Bourke. "Bart Flaherty is expecting you, ma'am. I will take you and the maid there. The boy will follow later."

Owen helped his mother to her feet, for she was stiff after the long ride. Her gray eyes answered his anxious look reassuringly, but there were black smudges beneath them, and her shoulders drooped as she went towards the stairs. He sat down, burying his face in his hands, overcome with shame when he thought how much he would add to her burden, when she learned he had failed her. Suddenly a way out of the difficulty came to him. With his mother's safety assured, this was the time to go back and get the documents. He was glad that it was Sean who had remained with him. A boy would be more easily persuaded than a man.

"Sean."

"Are you mad? Don't you even know that names are never mentioned? There must be no talk here. Come, it's time to go." Taking Owen's arm he pulled him up and shoved him towards the stairs.

Owen started down, furious at this treatment. Who did Sean think he was to deal this way with Owen Bourke of Cloona? He would make a run for it when they reached the ground. But as they came into daylight at the foot of the stairs, he felt Sean's strong hand on his shoulder. Owen tried to pull away, but Sean only tightened his grip.

"Don't try any tricks on me." The low voice was threatening. "I'm charged with getting you to Bart Flaherty's and that I'll do, if I have to carry you."

Remembering how he had been flung across O'Cahane's shoulder in the hall of Cloona, Owen gave up. He had no desire to enter Bart's house in that ignominious way. It was enough, and more than enough, that there was no reprieve for him. As soon as he was alone with his mother, he would have to tell her that the documents were still at Cloona.

He glanced at Sean, who was hurrying along, his eyes darting quick glances at the few people in the narrow street. He stopped at a wooden door, flush with the street, and rapped twice. Two answering raps came from within the house. When Sean responded with three more, the door swung open. Pushing Owen ahead of him, Sean entered, pulling the door closed behind him.

And there was Bart Flaherty, hand outstretched to Owen, who could see his mother and Anna seated before the fire, drinking broth, while their damp clothing dried in the heat.

CHAPTER FIVE

Owen went quickly to sit on the bench beside his mother. She smiled at him, but before either spoke, Mrs. Flaherty came in with steaming bowls of broth for the two boys. Owen sipped his gratefully, shivering as he did so. He had not realized how cold and hungry he was.

Sean, squatting before the fire, downed his in a gulp, and stood up, saying, "I'll be off, now."

Bart, whose height and bulk dwarfed the tall youth, put a restraining hand on Sean's shoulder. "Not yet, lad. You're to stay here until dark."

Sean squirmed, as if to throw off the restraining hand, but Bart did not let go. Owen's lips twitched. Looking up, he saw the sheepish grin on Sean's face. Their glances met, as if they shared a private joke. Owen warmed towards Sean, who was no longer the superior creature, contemptuous of his smaller companion, but a boy in the hands of a man, who towered over him, as he did over Owen.

"If you say so, sir," Sean said respectfully.

Bart dropped his hand and turned to Mrs. Bourke. "You'll be wanting some rest now. My wife will take you to your room."

Mrs. Bourke rose obediently as Bart extended his arm. "We have so much to plan," she began.

But Bart said soothingly, "Later will do. Rest is what all of you need first."

Owen stood as they left the room, his mother leaning wearily on Bart's arm while Anna followed with Mrs. Flaherty. When they were gone, Owen turned eagerly to Sean who had stretched himself out full length before the fire. "When you leave, I'm going with you. I must get back to Cloona."

"Must you, indeed?" Sean sat up. "After all the trouble we had getting you away. Is it your traitor cousin you're wishing to join?"

"You know better than that," Owen replied quietly. He must not let Sean goad him into anger, for it was only with the boy's help that he could hope to return to Cloona.

Bart walked into the room saying, "Come, Master Owen, a bed is ready for you. I'll get you a pallet in a minute, Sean."

"No need to. Sure this floor is a lot softer than many places I've slept." He lay down again. As his head touched the floor, he winked at Owen before shutting both eyes, as if already asleep.

Owen, his heart lightened by that sign, followed Bart from the room and up a steep flight of stairs to a small room under the eaves. The narrow bed had been freshly made with soft linen sheets and warm blankets.

"Have a good sleep, now," Bart said as he turned to leave. "No knowing when you'll have the chance again."

"Thank you," Owen said suppressing a yawn. Left alone, he looked at the tempting bed. He was bone weary, but he did not believe he could sleep. He must get back to the room where Sean slept to make plans. A knock at the door startled him. "If you'll hand me your clothes, I'll hang them by the fire to dry." It was Mrs. Flaherty's voice. Owen hastily took off the despised gray frieze coat and trousers and the heavy brogans, and handed them through the partially opened door. When he had closed it, he stood shivering in his undersuit, wondering what he should do, for now he could not go out of the room. He might as well get into bed for the present. As he did so, he remembered that Sean was under orders not to leave the house until dark. There would be time enough. He lay in bed trying to plan how he would get into the hidden room when he got to Cloona. He would have to let Patrick into the secret. His resourcefulness would find a way, Owen reflected, as the warmth of the blankets penetrated his tired body and he fell asleep.

When he awoke, the light had almost faded from the small patch of sky visible through the room's one window. For a moment he did not know where he was. When recollection flooded in, he got hastily out of bed and began to put on the dried suit which had been placed neatly on a chair while he slept. He was grateful for that, for he must see Sean before he left the house, which he doubtless would do as soon as night fell. Owen opened the door. The only sound from below seemed to come from the kitchen. Fortunately the passage at the foot of the stairs opened into the room where he had left Sean sleeping. He picked up the brogans which had been set beside the chair. He would carry them, he decided, hoping no one would hear him going down the stairs.

Sean still lay before the fire in the abandonment of sleep. Owen went quietly to the bench beside the hearth and sat down to put on his shoes. As he did so, he realized that Sean was watching him through almost-closed eyelids.

"You're awake, then."

Sean sat up, clasping his bony hands around his knees.

"Sure the first creak of the bed above wakened me. You'll have to do better than that, if you want to join the rapparees."

"Join the rapparees? What put that into your head?"

"For what else do you want to go back? It'd be the making of you."

"But I can't do that." Owen forgot to lower his voice, but at an impatient frown from Sean, dropped it, as he tried to explain. "I left something that I must get before I go to France. I thought you'd help me."

"O'Cahane'd kill me. If you'd tell me what and where it is, I might be able to get it for you."

Owen shook his head. "You'd have to know the house," he said. "You've got to help me, Sean. We could go now while no one is around. Once outside the walls, we could get the horses where we left them this morning. If we rode fast, we could be back here by dawn."

"And why did you leave this important thing behind in the first place?"

Owen's face burned with shame. "What does that matter? What's certain is I must go back. There's no time to lose."

Sean got to his feet and stood looking down at Owen. "And I say it's impossible. Believe me, Owen, it's the truth that I'm telling you. O'Cahane'd kill me, or at least he'd turn me out of the rapparees. His discipline is as strict as that of an army and more. I'd like to help you —" Stopping abruptly he turned towards the outer door. Looking in the same direction, Owen saw the latch being raised, though he had heard no sound to alert him. Sean walked quickly, but without making a sound, towards the kitchen door, beckoning Owen to follow. As Owen picked up the brogans on the bench beside him, one slipped from his grasp, clattering to the floor. As it did, the door opened and a tall man, wrapped in a long cloak, walked in followed by Bart, who quietly closed the door behind him. The first man removed his cloak, revealing beneath it the same peasant's frieze as the others wore, but Owen guessed it was as much a disguise as his own. When the man turned, Owen saw the tonsured head of a priest.

"Come here, lads," Bart said with a smile. "I'm sorry to have startled you, but a man doesn't think, coming into his own house. This is Father D'Arcy, who has come to help us."

When they had bowed to the priest, Bart said, "It's time for you to be off, Sean, though you'd best have a bite of supper first."

"A drink of milk and some bread is all I need."

"You'll find that and more in the kitchen. I'll join you in a minute, then see you over the wall."

"There's no need for that. I can find my way."

"My orders are to go with you."

Seeing Sean's nod of submission, Owen remembered the remark about O'Cahane's discipline. Sean had learned not to dispute it.

"Come to the fire and warm yourself, Father," Bart was saying, "I'll have Mrs. Flaherty rouse Mrs. Bourke."

"Let the poor woman have her sleep. I'll talk with the lad here while you're gone."

Father D'Arcy sat on the bench, motioning Owen to take the place beside him. "Why not put the shoes on, Owen? You don't need to be without them here."

Owen bent to the task, glad to be occupied. He felt as awkward and tongue-tied as any peasant. When he straightened up, Bart came from the kitchen, followed by Sean, who had a crusty loaf of bread in one hand. He waved good-bye to Owen with the other as he and Bart went through the outer door. Owen sighed as his only hope of getting back to Cloona vanished with Sean into the night.

"What troubles you, Owen?" The priest's voice was gentle but compelling. Owen looked into the kind eyes and noted the firm lines around the mouth, even when the lips were parted in a smile. Here was a man to whom he could confide his secret.

Falteringly Owen began, telling about the deed and his mother's placing the papers in his charge. He looked into the fire as he told of his failure, caused by his childish and shameful impulse. He felt he could conceal nothing from this man. There was silence when he had finished. Owen could not bring himself to meet the priest's gaze until the latter asked, "Could your cousin easily find this hiding place?"

"I thought I knew every inch of Cloona, yet never suspected it was there."

"It would seem that, if Hugh is aware of the existence of the deed, he would assume you had taken the papers with you. He is unlikely to suspect they are still in the house unless you give him reason to."

"You mean his suspicions would be aroused if he got wind of my still being in the neighborhood?"

Father D'Arcy nodded.

"But," Owen began again, "I can't go to France without the papers. How would I ever come back to get them?"

"Ever? Then you have no confidence in a victorious army returning from France? You are young to take a hopeless view."

"And you, Father? Do you look for their return?"

"I do not know, Owen. That we must leave to the Providence of God." He was silent for a while, his gaze fixed on Owen until he began to feel uncomfortable.

"Has this experience taught you to control your temper?"

"It could not do otherwise." Owen felt the warm flush of shame on his face, as Father D'Arcy said, "I too go to France soon. I shall return here in the spring, whether or not the army does. A boy your age could be a useful companion."

"You mean I could come back—" Owen broke off at a warning touch of the priest's hand. His mother was standing in the doorway. She looked strange and awkward in the tight bodice and short skirt of a peasant, but she walked towards them with a grace that suggested the long flowing skirts she was accustomed to wearing. Behind her, Mrs. Flaherty summoned them to supper. The tempting smell of roast lamb came from the hearth as they obeyed her call.

When Father D'Arcy had said Grace and they were seated on each side of the long table, Mrs. Bourke turned to Bart. "This morning you said you could arrange for us to sail for France. I hope it may be soon, for I would not trespass on your hospitality any longer than is absolutely necessary."

"You are most welcome guests. Were it safe for you to remain here, I would insist on it, rather than expose you to winter storms at sea, but I and all your friends will breathe easier when you are out of Ireland."

"Have you thought what you will do when you arrive in France?" Father D'Arcy asked the question gently.

"Only that I will go to Paris to Monsieur and Madame Castillon. They are old friends of my husband's. They will help me, I know, and Owen's uncle, Richard Bourke, will be glad to take the boy into his regiment."

Father D'Arcy studied her quietly before he spoke. "Your parents are still in England? How do they fare there?"

"I last heard from them in November. All was well with them when they wrote."

"Had you thought of going to them instead of to France?"

Seeing his hope of joining his uncle vanish with that suggestion, Owen could not suppress crying out, "Oh, no, not to England!" His mother smiled indulgently as she replied. "I think Owen is right. England is no place for him. My father's estate will go to a Protestant heir. What future would there be for Owen, then? And, under English law, Hugh Bourke could easily assert his claim as legal guardian and bring Owen back to Ireland, even during my father's lifetime."

"I was not thinking of Owen, but of you. France *is* the place for him."

As Mrs. Bourke understood what was meant, her hands grasped the edge of the table for support. The compassionate voice went on. "I know this is hard saying, Mistress Bourke, but these are difficult times. You have said truly that England is no place for the boy. I say that France is equally no place for you. Do you know what it is like at the Court of St. Germain? Since the Irish defeat, King James has only the bounty of King Louis to depend on. The palace is full of those who have followed the King into exile, and he is hard put to it to feed them. The generosity of those Irish, like the Castillons, who have lived long in France, is overtaxed. None but soldiers, or potential soldiers, like Owen, are welcome now. I cannot encourage your going to France, when you have a secure refuge in England."

Mrs. Bourke asked, in a voice that trembled in spite of her effort to control it, "And what of Owen? Would you have him make the journey to France alone and seek his uncle in an unknown country, without friends?"

"I would manage," Owen said confidently. "But what of you? How could you get to England with only Anna for a companion?"

Father D'Arcy smiled at Owen as he said, "Let us take one thing at a time. You understand my reason for urging you to go to England?" he asked Mrs. Bourke.

Before she answered, Bart broke in: "There is one advantage I can see in this madam. Hugh will be looking for two women and a boy. Separated, you are less likely to be found."

Mrs. Bourke gave him a grateful look. "You make the decision easier, since you think it will be safer that way. If it can be arranged, I will bow to your judgment, Father. I would indeed be glad to see my parents again." Her lips trembled.

To Owen, his English grandparents, whom he had never seen, were remote beings. He had forgotten that they were almost as dear to his mother as he was.

"I shall sail for France in a day or two," Father D'Arcy continued, "I will gladly take Owen with me. I only await word from *L'Esperance.*"

"A French ship?" Owen asked. "I thought they could no longer come to Limerick."

"No more they do," Bart spoke up. "But there are still bays in Kerry where a French privateer can put in."

"A privateer? But that will be dangerous," Mrs. Bourke protested.

Father D'Arcy looked reprovingly at Bart, but it was to Mrs. Bourke that he spoke. "There is danger ev-

74

erywhere for you and the boy, madam. But the captain of *L'Esperance* is an Irishman who knows these waters well. The vessel is fast and well armed. I've no doubt we'll arrive at St. Malo without incident. From there, I go to Paris and then to Rome, on a secret mission. I can easily arrange for Owen to go from St. Malo to his uncle's regiment, wherever it is stationed."

Owen, who had been saddened by the thought of separating from his mother, felt his spirits rise. To join Uncle Richard's regiment—maybe to be a cadet under him.

The priest continued. "I would like to make a suggestion. Let me take Owen to the Franciscan House of Studies in Paris, where other Irish and English boys are being educated. A year or two there would not be too costly, and he will be better prepared for whatever the future holds, be it the life of a soldier or some other calling."

"Oh no!" Owen could not check the exclamation.

Raising his eyebrows questioningly, Father D'Arcy said, "You would not like that? It might prove more interesting than you think."

Embarrassed that he had forgotten about his hope to return to Cloona, which would not be possible if he went into the army, Owen murmured "I'll do whatever my mother thinks best."

"Thank you, Owen. You make it easier for me. Your uncle may be disappointed, but your father would have preferred you to have more education before joining the army. I only ask," she turned to Father D'Arcy, "that you let Richard know as soon as possible. Owen is very dear to him."

"Richard Bourke is no stranger to me, madam. He was Owen's age when I knew him in France. He will be agreeable to your wishes, I've no doubt."

"Now, about your going to England, madam," Bart began. "I think it unsafe for you to attempt to get passage from Limerick. It would be better to go to Cork, or even Dublin, and take ship there. O'Cahane will gladly arrange an escort."

Owen saw the look of distress on his mother's face. He could not imagine her traveling across Ireland, guarded by rapparees, however grateful she might be for their help in escaping from Cloona.

Father D'Arcy came to her rescue. "I couldn't agree with you more as a general proposition, Bart. But I saw the brig, *Prince Edward,* at the quay today. She will sail with the morning tide. Her captain is a good friend of mine, though he is in the pay of the English." He stood up. "Let me go to him now. I'm sure you will have safe passage with him, madam. It may be that you should go aboard tonight. You had better be prepared when I return." He looked around the room. Realizing that he wanted his cloak, Owen went to the other room to get it. Returning, he placed it around the priest's shoulders. As he did so, Father D'Arcy murmured, "Say nothing about the missing papers, if you can avoid it." After wrapping his cloak around him, Father D'Arcy followed Bart through the room which opened onto the back street.

Mrs. Flaherty, who had quietly attended to the serving and removal of the food, with Anna's help, asked if there were anything she could get them.

"If I could have paper and ink," Mrs. Bourke replied,

"I would like to have Owen take a letter to the Castillons. While I write, Anna, you had better get the saddlebags from the room where we slept."

Mrs. Flaherty brought the requested articles and withdrew to leave mother and son alone. It was a moment Owen dreaded. If she asked him, should he deceive her, let her believe that he did have the documents in his coat? Father D'Arcy had not counseled that.

His mother did not speak for a moment. Turning away from him she had unbuttoned the front of her gown. Facing him again, she held in her hand the leather bag she had shown him only yesterday. "Let me have your purse, Owen. I shall take enough gold to get Anna and me to my father's house. The rest of it and my jewels you will take to France. Once there, you will give them to Monsieur Castillon, with the documents, for safekeeping." She counted the coins in Owen's purse, took a few from the bag, and handed it to him.

"You will have sufficient to take care of your expenses for a year, maybe longer. I do not want you to be a burden to Richard." Her eyes filled, but she brushed the tears away. "Now the letter. The Castillons will befriend your father's son, I know."

She picked up the quill pen and began to write. As Owen sat beside her, watching her hands as the pen scratched across the paper, he recalled what he knew of these Castillons. Like the Bourkes, they had gone to France in Cromwell's time, but had remained in Paris after the Restoration. He remembered his father saying that his friend Charles, a successful banker, had married a French woman. Owen remembered Uncle Richard saying that Charles had become as French as the family name, which unlike that of the Bourke's, had not changed in the long years since their Norman forebears arrived in Ireland.

His mother did not look up or speak until she had finished writing and carefully sanded the paper. She handed the folded paper to Owen. "I shall like to think of you at the Castillon's, in the familiar rooms where I first met your father."

"I shall not be able to picture the place where you are, Mother." They had never been separated before. Owen flung his arms around her, choking on the words he wanted to say. He also felt more certain than ever that he could not tell her of his failure to take the grant. Somehow he would find a way to retrieve it. At the sound of voices in the next room, his mother gently withdrew from his embrace. Owen stood up as Bart entered.

"Father has returned," he announced. "You and Anna must go with him at once."

Taking his mother's hand, Owen walked with her into the other room. Anna came from the passageway carrying the saddlebags and cloaks.

"All is arranged," Father D'Arcy told them. "Bart and I will take you to the brig now. Only the captain is on board. You will have his cabin. No one else will know of your presence until morning, when the *Prince Edward* is well down the Shannon."

Neither Owen nor his mother spoke, as they again embraced. After thanking Mrs. Flaherty for her kindness, Mrs. Bourke followed the two men and Anna through the door while Owen watched, his vision blurring as the door closed.

CHAPTER SIX

Owen stood in the bow of the privateer, *L'Esperance.*
The morning sun was dissolving the fog which had
shrouded the shores of France.

"There lies St. Malo!" A passing sailor stopped to
point out the gray promontory with its surrounding islands. The rocky coast advanced towards them as the
mist receded. Owen thought of the low green banks of
the Shannon where it flowed from Limerick to the sea.
It was as different from the scene before him as his old
life was from the new one that awaited him.

A small boat with a single sail put out from the shore,
heading for *L'Esperance.* On the deck behind Owen sailors hurried about in obedience to the captain's shouted
orders. A hand on his shoulder startled him. He turned
to find Father D'Arcy at his side. "It's time to come
below, lad. Captain Riordon prefers that we keep out of
sight when the pilot boards the ship."

Owen frowned with annoyance as they went below.
For the ten days since they had sailed from Ireland into

the wintry Atlantic, he had guarded every word and action. Before they embarked, he had been told that Father D'Arcy would be known to all on board as John Haley, a recruit for the Irish army, and Owen as his son. Only when they were in the cabin which the Captain shared with them, could they speak other than their native Gaelic, which the French sailors did not understand. Only once had Owen been surprised into replying in French to a remark by one of them, and that lapse had apparently been forgotten. But surely the need for so much caution had passed now that they were in the harbor of St. Malo. Within the cabin, Owen flung himself on the bunk.

"It is too bad you must miss the excitement of the ship docking," Father D'Arcy said quietly, "but there is still need for vigilance."

"I could understand while we were on the open sea and might be overtaken by an English man-of-war. I would not run the risk of being handed over to Hugh Bourke, but surely that danger has passed."

"True, but there are other considerations which have weighed more heavily with Captain Riordon and with me."

"Of course, Father, I realize that your safety comes first. But is not St. Malo a haven for you, too?"

"Yes, Owen, but it is most important that the Captain's purpose in making this voyage be not known. The business of a privateer is to intercept and capture the merchantmen of the enemy. This time he has no prize to bring into port; he has avoided any encounter with the English. Fog and storm played into his hands, but his crew are disappointed. They would not be happy if they knew he had sailed from France to Ireland and back solely to bring me here."

"But he has brought in recruits before. He told us so. Was not their safety important?"

"They took their chance. Even if captured, they would be no great prize for the English. With me it is different. For that reason it is much better if the crew and the people of St. Malo believe that we are the same as the others. Certainly, if any English spies are about, they will not be much alarmed at the kind of recruits that are being added to the Irish troops: an old man," he touched his graying hair, "and a beardless youth."

"But they take boys my age. If it were not for the hope of returning to Ireland with you, I would never have consented to the school in Paris. My mother would have allowed me to join Uncle Richard, if I had insisted."

"I know, Owen. It is natural that you should want to be a part of that army which every Irishman hopes and prays will restore our land to us. But the time may come when you will be glad that you were not."

"What do you mean, Father?"

The priest stood up. "I scarcely know myself, Owen. Just a feeling in my bones let us say. Listen! We are at the quay."

Above their heads there were shouts and running feet. A bump against the dock shook the vessel. Owen felt that he could not remain in the cabin a moment longer. As he stood up, the ship bumped again, throwing him across the bunk.

A sailor opened the hatchway above their heads. "The

captain asked me to tell you that an officer will come for you in an hour's time. Meanwhile, he wishes you to wait here."

"An hour will go quickly," Father D'Arcy said. "Have you everything ready?"

Owen put his hand on his saddlebag and the folded homespun cloak. "This is all I have."

"It is well. For we must continue as recruits until we are released, which I hope will be soon, for I must get to Paris without delay."

"Will I see Uncle Richard first? Captain Riordon said that most of the Irish troops are quartered somewhere in Brittany."

"Yes, it may be that Richard is near St. Malo. If so, you will surely see him while we are here."

Owen's joy at the prospect was quickly tempered. How would his uncle feel when he heard that his nephew was not going to join the army.

"You are wondering what Richard will say when you tell him your plans."

"Yes, Father. If only I could explain why."

"But that you cannot do, Owen. Not even Richard can know that I may return to Ireland."

"I understand. It will be hard, though, to hide my longing to stay with him."

"I know it is difficult. Still I feel the time will come when you will be glad of this decision."

"You said that before, Father. Don't you believe that the army will return to Ireland?"

"I do not claim the gift of prophecy. What the future holds, no man can know. But for a long time the tide has been running against the things that you and I have cherished. If I read history rightly, it has not reached its ebb and will not until the old kings and the old way of life have disappeared in this old world. I would urge you to claim your inheritance in the New World, where a new life awaits."

"First I have to get the grant before Hugh finds it." Owen remembered unhappily the distance he must travel back to Cloona.

"This I think you will accomplish." With this comforting remark, Father D'Arcy began to gather his few possessions.

It was not long before the hatchway was opened and Captain Riordon came down the companionway. "Mr. Fitzgerald, a lieutenant of the Irish Army, is on deck. He knows only that he is to meet two recruits to take to the camp outside the city."

"We are ready, Captain." Father D'Arcy stood up and Owen followed suit. "I am grateful for your kindness. May we meet again!"

"In an Ireland restored to its own—God speed the day!" The captain led the way to the ladder and the deck above. Coming into the sunlight which had burned away the earlier mist, Owen could not see the face of the officer, who stood with his back to the light. But his harsh voice rapped out the command to advance as if Owen and Father D'Arcy were recruits from the peasantry. Owen made no move to obey immediately although Father D'Arcy was already on his way across the gangplank.

"Get on with you, lad." The Captain's hand on Owen's

back pushed him forward. On the stone pier he caught up with Father D'Arcy who, finger to lip, stopped the indignant words before Owen could speak. He shivered in the cold wind that blew off the water, wishing he had wrapped his cloak around him. But to stop would invite further humiliation from Mr. Fitzgerald who, without a break in his quick pace, glanced around to see that his charges were following him. As they passed through the gateway in the stone rampart which surrounded the city, Owen noticed two men in its shadow. One, he was sure, was Henri, the sailor from *L'Esperance* to whom Owen had accidentally betrayed his knowledge of French. He glanced at Father D'Arcy to see if he had noticed the men, but his face was impassive, his head held erect, his eyes looking straight ahead, in imitation of a soldier on parade.

Walking on the cobbled street was not easy after the narrow confinement of the ship. Owen could no more than glance sideways at the tall stone houses which climbed by narrow crooked streets to the cathedral on the summit of the island. Already they were approaching another gate which led to the causeway joining the town to the mainland. Owen decided, this time, to wrap his cloak around him before leaving the sheltering rampart. He dropped the saddlebag he had been carrying and opened the cloak. As he put it around his shoulders, it was seized from behind and pulled over his head, binding his arms in its folds. He was lifted up. He could not cry out against the thick folds of the cloak. He kicked his captor as hard as he could. Nevertheless, strong arms held him tight. After a few steps he was set down hard on rough wood, its splinters pricking through his frieze trousers. The hands holding his arms moved downward, while other hands lifted the cloak above his mouth and nose so that he could breathe, but pulling it closely over his eyes. The hand gripping his left arm let go, but before Owen could move, an arm was hard against him, reaching across his chest to grasp his right arm. There was a movement of the cloak across his eyes, as the man behind him seized it, while the one leaning over him moved away.

"Now, speak up quickly," an unfamiliar voice said in his ear. "No harm will come to you if you answer our questions. The name of the man with you, what is it?"

The voice was not Henri's, so Owen muttered in Gaelic, "I do not understand."

"What did he say?" The questioner had an English accent. Owen could tell it came from in front of him.

"Henri said he spoke French," the other replied, "but not a word of that could I comprehend. Better try him in English."

So the question was repeated in English, but Owen shook his head, repeating the Gaelic phrase. Then he let his jaw drop, remembering how he had done it before the mirror in Cloona. If anything would, that should convince his captors that he did not know what they were saying.

"We waste our time," the English voice said impatiently. "Your friend, Henri, has told us a fine fairy tale to earn a few francs."

"But, no, monsieur," the voice behind Owen protested. "He may have been mistaken about the boy, but not the man."

"What goes on here?" At Mr. Fitzgerald's harsh voice the hands holding Owen let go so quickly that he almost fell. His cloak dropped behind him and he reached to pick it up as the officer spoke again. "Answer me. What are you doing to the boy? How dare you lay hands on one in the charge of an officer?"

Owen, cloak in hand, stood up, facing a doorway in which Mr. Fitzgerald stood, sword in hand. He blocked any light from entering the windowless enclosure, so Owen could not see more than light blobs which must have been the faces of his captors. From one of them came a voice which Owen recognized as that of the one who had held him.

"We did but have a little fun with the boy. We meant him no harm."

"Is this true, lad?" Mr. Fitzgerald asked.

In Gaelic Owen told him of the attempt to find out the real name of his companion and its failure.

"Scoundrels! I should turn you over to the guard."

"Not that, I beg you, monsieur. A flogging is a severe penalty for so slight an offence. You can see for yourself the boy is unharmed."

"Come out into the daylight, lad, so I can be certain of that," Mr. Fitzgerald commanded, moving to one side to let Owen go through the doorway. Satisfied that he was uninjured, Mr. Fitzgerald turned back to the two men. "I will let you go this time, but if ever again I find you harassing recruits of His Majesty's army you will not get off so easy." He stepped back, sword still in hand, as the two men came running out. Soon they were out of sight.

Turning to Owen, the officer said, as he sheathed his sword, "Those men should have been held. But I could not do that and obey my orders to bring you to camp with all speed. Had you not loitered behind me this would not have happened. The commander of the camp will hear about it. Pick up your saddlebag. Join your companion. You will march ahead of me so there will be no further incidents."

Owen did as he was told, though raging inwardly at the rebuke. Not a word of praise for what he felt had been a commendable performance. He walked through the gate and out onto the causeway beside Father D'Arcy. Beyond, through bare tree branches, he could see the camp.

When they came to the first sentry, Mr. Fitzgerald stepped forward to give the password. He then led them towards a tent, larger than the others, flying the standard of King James and the flag of France.

"You will wait here," he told them, "while I report to the Captain in charge."

And that, Owen hoped, was the last order he would receive from the hostile officer. Father D'Arcy stood at ease, but shook his head when Owen started to speak. So he waited, cold and impatient. A group of soldiers passed by, curiously inspecting the new recruits. Owen seethed under their scrutiny, then looked away as if unaware of it.

"You will come with me." Owen jumped at Mr. Fitzgerald's voice. He had not seen the officer come out of the tent into which he now led them. In the dim light Owen could not see clearly the man who sat behind a table, his head bent over the papers in front of him.

"These are the two men I have brought you from *L'Esperance*, John Haley and his son, Owen, Captain Bourke."

It was Uncle Richard. Owen's eager step forward was halted by his uncle's lifted palm and impassive face. The time for recognition had not come.

"You will leave the Haleys with me," Richard Bourke said to Mr. Fitzgerald. "They come from near my home and I wish to speak with them, alone."

"Very good, sir." Saluting, the officer turned to leave as his Captain rose and came forward to stand in front of Owen.

"Uncle Richard!" Owen's cry was muffled against his uncle's shoulder. It was almost like being at home to be held in those arms again.

When Owen raised his head, Richard put his hands on the boy's shoulders, saying, "What does this mean, Owen? Why are you here under a false name? And your companion?" He turned toward the priest.

"You do not recognize me?" Father D'Arcy removed his cap, exposing the tonsure. Richard studied the face for a moment, then said, "Father D'Arcy? Is it possible? It was in Paris when I was Owen's age that I last saw you."

"That's right. Isn't it strange that I should now be acting as guardian for your nephew?"

Feeling Richard's start of surprise, Owen hastened to

say, "My mother has gone to her parents in England and Father D'Arcy offered to bring me here."

"I must know what has happened. But, come let us sit down. He pulled Owen's chair close to his own, and the priest sat down on one of the camp chairs nearby. "I was not told who you were, Father, though I was ordered to send Mr. Haley on as soon as he arrived. You will go this afternoon. Now Owen, tell me everything."

When Owen told of the incident at the ship's gate, Richard said, "Mr. Fitzgerald praised your presence of mind, Owen, though he found you somewhat deficient in obeying orders. That you'll have to learn, for being the Captain's nephew will be no excuse for insubordination, once you are enrolled as a cadet in my regiment."

Owen stiffened against his uncle's arm. His throat tightened so that he could hardly speak the words he had been dreading. "But, I'm not going to be—"

"What?" Richard withdrew his arm and turned so that he could look directly at Owen, who sat with his head down and his hands clasping his knees. This was the moment he had feared. Drawing a deep breath, he lifted his head to look directly at his uncle.

"I am not joining the army." Owen's voice was not quite steady. "I promised my mother I would go first for a year to the Franciscan House of Studies in Paris."

"So!" Richard shoved his chair back and got to his feet. His voice was harsh as he said, "You'll not be the first promising soldier to be spoiled by priests and women."

Owen stiffened at his uncle's scorn. "It is what my father would wish. Besides—" He stopped in time to keep from blurting out his desire to return to Cloona.

But Richard had not noticed. "It is what your mother thinks your father would wish. I'm his brother. Believe me, he would want his son with the army when it returns to Ireland. I can only believe that stronger wills than yours have made this decision for you." He stopped abruptly, turning away from Owen.

"I have given my word, Uncle Richard. I cannot break it."

"Nor can I urge you to." After a few unhappy minutes of silence, Richard resumed his seat. "Father, I must ask your pardon for my hasty words. I was angry that Margaret had not allowed me some part in plans for Owen's future. Since that is not to be, I am happy that he will be in your charge."

"Thank you, Richard. I shall not be in Paris long. However, Owen has a letter from his mother to Monsieur Castillon, who will, I'm sure, interest himself in his old friend's son."

"Of course. Have you anything else to deliver to Monsieur Castillon, Owen?"

"Mother's jewels and all the gold she had, except what she needed for her journey to England."

"That is all?"

"Yes." Owen felt he could read his uncle's thoughts that Margaret Bourke had considered her son too young to be charged with responsibility for the Maryland grant. He was glad his uncle did not have to know the truth.

"If you are going to Paris, you will have to go this

afternoon," Richard said, a little sadly, "for Father's departure cannot be delayed. We'll dine together here in my tent so let's be merry while we may."

CHAPTER SEVEN

The April air brushed Owen's cheek as he sat in the window seat of his chamber in the Castillon house. The scent of spring it carried from the fields and forests beyond the city wall increased his restlessness.

Yesterday Owen had been summoned to Monsieur Castillon's house. When he arrived there from the Franciscan House of Studies, Monsieur had told Owen that his mother was safely with her parents in England.

"As I told you, I would, when you first came to Paris, I made inquiries through my banking correspondent in Antwerp. He requested his associate in England to make inquiries," Monsieur had said. He had given no further explanation for summoning Owen.

Although Owen was happy to hear this, he felt certain that it was not the only reason for his being here. Did it mean that Father D'Arcy was returning from Rome?

Owen got up to stride about the narrow room, almost half of which was occupied by the canopied bed. He stood at the window, looking down at the muddy street three stories below. While he watched, a coach turned into the narrow Rue St. Etienne and stopped before the great door of the Castillon residence. The groom jumped down from the box to open the door. As the traveler, dressed in rich black, stepped out, he looked up. There was something familiar in the tilt of the head, but the white wig under the plumed hat suggested only another caller for his host. Owen turned away in disappointment as the man entered the house.

Flinging himself down on the windowseat, he stared at the patch of blue which he could see above the tall houses across the street. Longing for the open fields of Cloona, with the wide sky over them, stirred in him. With closed eyes he imagined them, covered with the fresh green of April, starred with daisies, surrounded with flowering hawthorne hedges, in the distance the gleaming Shannon water. A knock at the door startled him.

"Come in."

A footman in black and gold livery entered. "Monsieur desires your presence in the library."

"I'll come immediately." Owen took a moment to brush his hair so that it hung neatly to the lace collar of his coat. Perhaps the traveler had brought news from Rome, good news he hoped, as he hurried down the two flights of stairs and along the wide hall to the library. A footman opened the door, announcing, "Monsieur Owen."

"Owen, my son!" In the room, darkened by heavy draperies, Owen could not see the priest, but there was no mistaking his voice.

"Father," Owen ran to him. "You are here at last."

"Has it seemed so long? It is but ten weeks since I left you!"

"But such a long ten weeks! Truly, the longest of my life!"

"As bad as that!" The priest drew Owen down on the sofa beside him. "You have not been happy in Paris?"

"The time has gone so slowly. I am no great student, you know, and I've missed the free ways of Cloona, especially now that spring is here. Sometimes it has seemed as if I couldn't bear to be confined in the city, without even a horse to ride."

With a smile, Father D'Arcy said, "You will not be sorry, then, to learn that I am soon to go to Ireland."

"And you will take me with you? I've been wondering why Monsieur had me come here, but he did not explain."

"He is very discreet. He could not be certain until I arrived. Praise be to God, arrangements are now complete. You see before you, my lad," he stood up to display his velvet suit, with lace at the neck and wrists, "not Father D'Arcy, but Mynheer Jacob Van der Groate, and you will be my son, Jan. As such we shall sail from Antwerp to Dublin in two weeks. Meanwhile," he went on, forestalling the question forming on Owen's lips, "you will visit your uncle for a week. So you will continue to be Owen Bourke until you leave the Irish camp."

"But Uncle Richard wrote me two weeks ago that the invasion would start soon. Will the army still be in camp?"

"Yes. They wait for the Mediterranean fleet to join Tourville's at Havre du Grace. There will be time. You will go tomorrow. Monsieur will send his servant Jacques with you."

"Then," Owen said, his face lighting up, "I can tell Uncle Richard of my going and he will know why I have stayed in Paris instead of joining the army?" For delighted as he was at the prospect, he was not sure of his reception as a visitor. Uncle Richard might not be very proud to have a nephew who was a student in Paris, not a member of the invading force.

"No, Owen, you may not tell your uncle of our plan. Not that I don't trust him, but it is a secret to be shared only with those essential to accomplish it. In France they are only Monsieur and Jacques. I do not even go to the house of our order in Paris, for it is not Father D'Arcy who has traveled from Rome but, as I told you, Mynheer Van der Groate, who visits his friend and associate, Monsieur Castillon."

"Then there really is such a person?"

"Most certainly, and I travel with his papers while he remains in seclusion in Rome. You see, Owen, that is why you are going to the camp. You could not travel from Paris with me, for Mynheer's son is in Brussels. You will meet me at Antwerp, while your schoolfellows will understand that you have gone to join your uncle's regiment. So you must tell Richard nothing. I know that will not be easy for you, but there is much at stake, for you as well as for me." He smiled at the boy's anxious face. "I have confidence that you will keep our secret."

"Of course I will, though I'm afraid Uncle Richard may not be happy to see me in a camp where hundreds my age are training to be soldiers."

"Monsieur will be able to help you there. He will give you letters to Richard and others at the camp. Now we must join our host, so that he may give you more detailed instructions."

Reluctantly Owen followed the priest into the hall and across it to the small sitting room where Monsieur and Madame Castillon waited for them. He never felt entirely at ease with his father's friend who, like his name, seemed more French than Irish. Though both he and his wife had warmly welcomed James Bourke's son, the rigid order of their household oppressed Owen. He was more homesick for Cloona here than among the boys at the Franciscans. He drew a long breath as he entered the room. How good it would be to get away to the camp and then to Ireland!

The shadows lay long across the grass three days later when Owen and Jacques rode toward the Irish camp. The standard of King James rippled in the breeze which blew in from the Channel. Owen shivered with excitement. Uncle Richard was somewhere among those white tents, or out on the parade ground where a troop of cavalry in bright red coats were pacing their horses.

At the gate, Owen handed the sentry the pass which Monsieur had given him. Having examined the paper, the sentry called a passing soldier, instructing him to take Owen and Jacques to Captain Bourke.

As they rode between the rows of tents, fires were burning here and there. Soldiers were hurrying toward them, drawn by the smell of roasting meat which the light breeze blew across the camp. Owen noticed how well clothed and equipped the men were. Then he saw a group of them come to attention as a tall man wearing a long, black wig came riding towards them on a roan horse. He tossed a word of greeting to the silent soldiers, who smiled delightedly as they watched him ride towards the tent from which floated the king's banner. "Who is he?" Owen asked his escort. "Patrick Sarsfield, Earl of Lucan," was the answer; and Owen understood the affectionate awe of the men who had been addressed.

Approaching the encampment of the cavalry regiments, Owen forgot even Sarsfield in his joy. The soldier leading them drew rein before a tent. An orderly stepped out to be handed the pass. He took it inside. In a second his uncle appeared, exclaiming, "Owen! What fair wind blew you here?"

Instantly Owen was off his horse. His arm around his uncle, he answered, "Monsieur Castillon sent me with Jacques. The letters we bring will explain everything. He was so kind to give me this opportunity to see you."

Richard looked questioningly at his nephew. Then calling his servant to look after Jacques and the horses, he led Owen into his tent, saying, "I must hear all about what you have been doing."

Two days later at the same hour, Owen and his uncle stood on the heights at La Hogue looking down over the bay where Tourville's fleet rode at anchor. The French had assembled a proud array of ships, though they were not considered powerful enough to defeat the Dutch and

English fleets combined, Richard was explaining to Owen. "We're still awaiting the fleet from the Mediterranean to join this one. Together they should be more than a match for anything William can bring against them. I understand," he lowered his voice cautiously, "that the King is confident the English will come over to him when the French ships sail out. The Marechal de Bellefonds, who is military commander under the King, is not so sure."

"Do you think they will?" Owen asked as he looked down at the ships lying idle, their sails furled. In the clear light he could see moving figures on the decks, while now and then a small boat put out from the harbor and headed towards the fleet.

"I wish I could believe it," Richard answered slowly, "but I do not trust the enemy. Those same men turned against King James four years ago. Why should they turn to him now unless they have tired of the Dutchman? I put my faith in the French fleet. If it can clear the Channel for us, I believe our army can conquer England. If James gains England, Ireland will be ours. Then you will return to Cloona. But we must go back to the camp; it's time to eat."

As Owen walked towards the encampment, his hopes rose. Surely this army, thirty thousand strong, could vanquish the English and the Dutch, and return as deliverers to Ireland. Perhaps he would not come back to France at all, for the war might be over while he was still in Ireland. How surprised his uncle would be to find him there!

"How proud I would have been to have you as a

soldier in my company when it marched in triumph —
But look!" Uncle Richard said.

Owen saw Patrick Sarsfield striding towards them.

Uncle Richard saluted and Owen stood with hat in
hand as the great man approached. He was even larger
than he had appeared on horseback. Uncle Richard
looked a mere stripling beside the Earl, who greeted him
warmly, then turned his deep blue eyes to look down at
Owen.

"So you are James Bourke's son!" His smile was sweet,
lighting up a face that had been stern and melancholy in
repose. "I knew your father well. I would that he were
with us now. We have need of such men. Please God, this
summer will prove that he and others have not died in
vain."

Owen could only gaze in awe at this man who was
already a legend among the Irish. He looked a hero, the
boy thought, with his commanding stature, the fire in his
blue eyes as he spoke of his hopes, the firm, resolute jaw,
the lips that could smile so graciously. Owen's heart beat
fast as he took the proffered hand. Then the Earl left
them. Owen and his uncle stood silently for a minute
watching the red-coated figure move away.

"A great man," Richard said softly. "I wish he had
command of the army."

"Why doesn't the King give it to him?"

"As long as we have to rely on the French king for
money and supplies, we shall have French officers leading us. Too, I suspect that the Englishmen around James
still assume that the Irish are inferior, even those like the

Sarsfields and the Bourkes who have tainted their Norman blood by intermarrying with the mere Irish."

"Small wonder if they take the likes of Hugh Bourke as representative," Owen said.

But his uncle's thoughts were still on Sarsfield. "There's a man who understands the Irish terrain and the Irish fighting man, too. Remember how he blew up the English artillery train at Ballyneety two summers ago?"

"Patrick told me about it the next day, for it shook the windows at Cloona that night. Were you there, Uncle?"

"Yes, I was indeed. Five hundred men on horseback slipped out of Limerick at night, across Thomond Bridge into Clare, although the English thought their siege lines would prevent any from leaving. Sarsfield planned it all. We rode through Clare to the ford at Killaloe. There we crossed the river and hid all the next day on the side of Keeper Mountain, although the English were patrolling the road where the artillery train was to pass. They camped that night at Ballyneety. When it was dark, we rode into their camp so quickly and quietly that they did not know we were there until the first wagon of ammunition was blown up. And Sarsfield there in the thick of it, directing the action and hurrying the men off again as soon as the task was accomplished. He forced the English to abandon the first siege of Limerick. Do you know who was the chief scout that night? Your friend, O'Cahane!"

CHAPTER EIGHT

Owen stood at the window, looking out at the rain pouring from the gray sky onto the gray roofs of Dublin. Two weeks had passed since he had left the sunlit Irish camp on the French coast. For three days he had been practically a prisoner in this room. For on their arrival at the Carbrie, Father D'Arcy and Owen had learned that Hugh Bourke was also at the inn. So Owen, as Jan Van Der Groate, had to feign illness, while Father D'Arcy as Mynheer, went daily about the business which had brought him from Antwerp.

Depressed by the monotonous beating of the rain, Owen went to lie down again. Paris had been better than imprisonment in this strange city which was not the Ireland for which he had longed. As he wondered how he could stand another day's confinement, the door opened and Father D'Arcy came in.

"What news, Father? Has Hugh left the city?"

"He is still here, Owen, but you and I are leaving before dawn tomorrow."

"Tomorrow?" Owen sat up. "I thought we were staying here another week."

"That was the plan." The priest sat down beside Owen, his voice low-pitched. "There is more I should do here, as you know. But someone has become suspicious. There is danger that the authorities may penetrate our disguise; so Mynheer Van der Groat and his son will depart in the morning. Mynheer, having business in Belfast, will take his son to visit with his friends, the Purcells, in Kildare."

"You mean we aren't going on together? How shall I pretend to be Jan with people who know him? When am I going to Limerick?"

"Keep your voice down, Owen. What I say is for you alone." Father D'Arcy drew his chair closer to the bed. "Before daylight we will set out by coach on our way to Kildare. About an hour and a half out of the city, we will drive along a road with high hedgerows on either side. At a point where it is barely wide enough for the coach to pass, the horses will slow almost to a stop. You will get out and disappear quickly through a gap in the hedge. Do not look back. Go directly to the farmhouse you will see a little way off."

"But—" Owen began.

"Owen, please. Your safety may depend on your doing exactly as I say. The door will be open. You will go in, closing it softly, and walk across the floor until you stand in the full light from the window. Taking off your hat, you will wait. A man will be standing by the hearth. You will not speak until he speaks to you."

"It sounds like the rapparees."

"Yes. Thank God for the rapparees. From there on you will be under their protection until you are again at Cloona."

"And you, Father? Where are you going? When shall I see you again?"

"In Limerick, I trust, after you have been to Cloona. For I shall be crossing Ireland by a longer road." He walked over to look out the window.

Owen lay gazing at the ceiling in the darkening room, his thoughts reaching across the miles to Cloona, where the Maryland papers still waited in the hidden room. He would not believe that Hugh had found them. Perhaps it was fortunate that they were leaving Dublin while his cousin was still here. Owen realized that it was fortunate only for him. For Father D'Arcy, who had not completed his work, it was a disappointment.

Owen got out of bed and went across the room to stand beside Father D'Arcy. "What of your mission here? Will you return later?"

"The future is in God's hands, Owen. I hope and pray that I may be able to come back, for otherwise I shall have failed to finish what I was sent to accomplish." He sighed, continuing to look out the window. In the deepening gray, the street below was almost deserted. Many of the houses were shuttered. The city seemed forlorn and empty in the driving rain.

"How different from the last time I was in Dublin." He turned away from the window. "It was the day King James entered the city. The sun was shining. High Street, so empty now, was lined with crowds. Flags hung from every window. As far as one could see, from the gate to the castle up on the hill marched the soldiers escorting the King, the flower of the Irish Army that was to drive the enemy out. And that but three years ago."

"My father was here that day," Owen said. "He rode with Sarsfield's troop of horses."

"Yes, he and many another good man who gave up their lives in vain."

There was a knock at the door. Owen hastened back to the bed so as to appear the invalid he was supposed to be, when the waiter came in with the evening meal.

"This is welcome," Father D'Arcy said, when the man had left. "I think hunger is responsible for some of our melancholy. Eat well, Owen, for you will need strength for tomorrow."

As he dressed in the dark next morning, Owen's pleasure at the thought of getting away from the inn, which had been a prison to him, was forgotten. The imminent parting from Father D'Arcy with his mother in England, and Uncle Richard in France, would leave him to make his way alone. Doubtless the rapparees would take him safely across Ireland, but he would be more alone than he had ever been before, among those silent men.

Supported by Father D'Arcy's arm, Owen walked through the passageway to the waiting coach. The arm was given, he knew, to continue the fiction of his illness, but it was his spirit that needed support. He wanted to beg the priest not to leave him; to take him into whatever danger lay ahead. Though he felt that the separation had been planned for his safety, he did not want to be safe while his only friend was in peril. But he must follow the plan laid out for him and not distress Father D'Arcy by any sign of faltering.

As the coach jolted along, Owen could see nothing of the city in the predawn darkness. Then the carriage stopped.

"We are at the gate," Father D'Arcy said in answer to Owen's questioning glance. There was the clang of iron, then the coach started up. "I'm glad we're through. No alarm has been given."

As the horses began to run along the open road, Owen could see a line of light along the horizon. Dawn was coming and with it a note of cheerfulness. Whatever the day held, at least he was on his way toward the west and home.

The horses slowed as they turned into a narrow lane with hedgerows high on either side. Father D'Arcy settled back in the seat. "I'm relieved we are off the high road. All should go as planned." He closed his eyes and, in spite of the jolting of the coach, was soon dozing.

Owen, too apprehensive to relax, noticed how lined the priest's face was. Seen in repose, it was the countenance of an old and weary man. For the first time, Owen knew fear that he might not see his friend again.

The coach made another sharp turn to the left, throwing Father D'Arcy against Owen's shoulder. As he opened his eyes, the horses slowed to a walk. His hand clasped Owen's.

"Are you ready?"

Owen nodded, finding no words with which to say

good-bye. Almost imperceptibly the coach stopped moving.

"God be with you!" Father D'Arcy said softly as Owen stepped out of the coach down into the road. Before him was the gap in the hedge through which he would go, casting no longing backward glance toward the coach whose wheels began to creak as it moved slowly away.

When Owen stepped through the gap, the sun was full in his face, blinding him for a moment. The scent of heather filled the air. Shading his eyes with his hand, Owen saw the bogland stretching before him, covered with the purple blossoms. A little way off to the right were the white walls and amber thatched roof of the farmhouse. He quickly picked his way over the hummocky path leading to it. A welcome thread of smoke coming from the chimney brought the rumblings of hunger to Owen's stomach.

Entering the open door, he stepped into a stone-paved kitchen. On the hearth a fire burned brightly and the smell of roasting chicken filled the air. First closing the door as he had been instructed, Owen walked across the floor until he stood in the full light from the window.

A tall, bearded man in the familiar gray frieze was standing by the hearth. He studied Owen carefully. As if I were a horse he might buy, Owen thought. When it seemed the silent scrutiny would go on forever, the man spoke, the Gaelic words sounding strange to Owen after so many months.

"In there," the man gestured towards a door on the

wall opposite him, "you'll find a change of clothing. Put them on and bring me those you are wearing."

In the room Owen found a worn, though clean suit of gray frieze. This time he was glad to take off his fine Paris suit which had felt out of place in his walk across the bog. No one would recognize Jan Van der Groate, or Owen Bourke for that matter, in the peasant he would now appear.

His velvet suit exchanged for the frieze and his polished leather boots for the rough brogans, he went back to the kitchen. Still silent, in the way of his kind, the rapparee led Owen through another door into the buttery. Its walls were lined with shelves and cupboards. Stopping at the first cupboard, the man placed his finger at its angle with the wall. As he pressed gently against the wood, the whole cupboard swung out, revealing a hollow space large enough for a man to stand in. There was a small wooden chest on the floor. Lifting the lid, the rapparee motioned Owen to put his velvet suit inside. That done, the cupboard was swung back into place. From a shelf beyond, the man picked up a pitcher of milk, indicating to Owen that he was to take the round of butter and pot of honey beside it.

Back to the kitchen they went, placing the food on the oak table which stood before the hearth.

"Sit ye down." As Owen obediently sat on the settle, his companion went to the hearth and lifted a chicken from the pot oven. He brought it to the table on a wooden platter and carved it with the knife he wore in his belt. Then he took wooden bowls from the dresser, setting one in front of Owen. Going again to the hearth, he took slabs of oat cake from the fire and brought them to the table. Using his fingers, as he knew he must, Owen helped himself to the chicken.

When their silent meal was finished, the rapparee studied Owen for a moment, shaking his head. Then wiping his greasy knife on a piece of oat cake, he came over to Owen. "We'll have to get rid of that long hair," he said seizing the boy's head and hacking away at the long hair. So harsh was his method that Owen felt as if his hair were being pulled out by the roots. The cutting finished, the man ran his rough hands through the hair that was left. Standing back he looked approvingly at his handiwork.

"Sorry to hurt you, lad, but you have to look like Tim Feenan. From this moment on, that's your name and you recognize no other. You speak naught but Gaelic. When you walk out this door, you'll take the path in the opposite direction from the way you came. Through the hedgerow at the end, you'll find a horse tethered."

Owen wanted to protest at being sent on his way alone, but had learned the law of the rapparees; one obeyed orders and did not speak unless required to. The rapparee spread a rough map on the table. He pointed to a cross. "Here's where you'll find the horse. You'll mount and ride to the end. Then turn west on the high road." He indicated an arrow pointing in that direction. His finger followed the wobbly line across the paper. "It'll be evening when you come to the wall of a big house, covered with ivy it is. Not far beyond the gate, you'll see a cottage. You'll ride up to it and ask for the Widow Brown. Should any stop you on the road, that's where you're bound, do they ask you in your own tongue. Your home is back this way. You're returning her horse your father borrowed to help with the plowing. You've got that down have you?"

Owen nodded, as he reached for the map.

"No, lad." The man put it back in his pocket. "Tim Feenan knows the road well. And the old horse knows it better. Never fear you'll get there, if you keep your wits about you."

He walked towards the door. Leaning his back against it, he said, "Now let me see you walk across the floor as if you were used to working in the fields."

Owen stood up, wondering how that was. Then remembering the way of the men at home, he dropped his head forward, his eyes seeing only the floor boards as he walked towards the rapparee.

"You'll do fine, but your hands are too white and soft." The man stepped outside, Owen following. The rapparee stooped to rub his hands in the boggy soil. He quickly wiped them off on Owen's as the boy recoiled from the feeling of the muck. A faint smile touched the man's lips as he finished by running a couple of fingers down Owen's cheeks. Standing back, he nodded his head, saying, "You'll do, if none comes too close. Now be off."

Owen stood for a moment. Then gathering his courage in his two dirty hands he started across the bog. It was easy enough to keep his head down, for he had to watch his step, and the heavy brogans dragged at his feet. As he reached the hedge, he lifted his head a moment to the blue sky where a few clouds floated. He breathed deep of the air of Ireland.

Ducking through the hedge, he found the horse tied to a hawthorn bush. "And a poor excuse for a horse, you are," he said as he untied the animal. An old piece of blanket was all there was for a saddle and only a rope halter for a bridle. But Owen mounted with no fear that the poor old beast would be hard to handle. As they turned into the road which went towards Cloona, Owen smiled, remembering how last night he had dreamed of galloping across the land with the wind in his face. The poor creature beneath him plodded along, more accustomed, Owen was sure, to following the plow than carrying a rider. The horse's head hung down and his heavy hooves sank deep into the mud.

As they went, Owen caught occasional glimpses through the hedgerows of the boglands stretching away on either side. The sun was hot. His legs, hanging down with no stirrups to hold them, began to tingle, his head drooped forward, his hand slackened on the rough rope. He jerked awake just as he was sliding off the horse's back. He decided to dismount and walk for a bit. This way he was able to shake off the sleepy feeling which had almost overcome him. It was good to be off that bony seat, but the brogans hurt his feet and he began to feel a blister rising on one heel. So he climbed onto the horse again. As he did so, he noticed that the road was no longer flat, but rising gently. Through a gap in the hedge, he could see fields green with grass that sheep had nibbled. He must be approaching some estate, though it was too early in the day to look for the one near which dwelt the Widow Brown. He wondered if the rapparee knew how slow the old horse was when he had said Owen would reach there by evening.

The land was very still. Only the hum of insects or an occasional birdcall sounded. The sun was full in his face. The hedges were thinner so that he could see through them into pastures where cattle had browsed, and beyond, as the land rose gently towards southern hills, cultivated fields. Perhaps he had not much further to go, though he saw no dwelling. Then he heard behind him the sound of horses' hooves. They were coming fast. He was frightened. In this open country there was no place he could hide. Then he remembered there was no need to hide. He was Tim Feenan, on his way to the Widow Brown's. Whoever the riders were, they were no concern of his. He guided the old horse to the side of the road and turned to gape, as he felt Tim would, at the fine horses and glittering uniforms of the three men nearing him. They wore King William's colors.

To Owen's dismay, the riders halted when they came abreast of him. The one nearest him called out, in English, "Have you seen a coach pass this way?"

Owen rubbed one dirty hand across his face as he stared uncomprehendingly at the speaker.

"You ask him in his own tongue, Bourke."

Owen heard this with a stab of fear. He lowered his head, stroking his face so that the dried mud on his hand stuck to his sweat.

"I know little of it," his cousin Hugh's voice replied, "though one can't help picking up a word here and there from the peasants." Then he put the question haltingly in Gaelic. Owen shook his head as he answered truthfully, "No one has passed on this road." His voice came hoarsely from his throat, dry as much from fear as from the thirst he was suddenly conscious of.

"He's seen no one," Hugh reported to his companions. "Let us ride on. There's ease and refreshment to be had at Purcell's. And perhaps word of our quarry, too."

But the first speaker was not satisfied. "Find out first," he told Hugh, "who the boy is and where he is going. One never knows what mischief the natives may be up to."

Unwillingly Hugh obliged and Owen answered as he had been told to, but haltingly.

Hugh repeated the words in English so that his companion agreed there was nothing to be learned from this dullard. Then the three riders galloped off as if to make up for lost time.

Owen turned his horse into the road and plodded after them, wondering what he should do now. For Hugh Bourke to be in the immediate neighborhood for the night was the worst of bad luck. Hugh was not too bright, but he might later recall some look or feature of the boy on the road as resembling Owen, especially when the Purcells had no word of Mynheer Van der Grote and his son. Hugh's presence suggested that he already knew or suspected that Owen had been disguised as Jan.

Yet if he didn't stop at the Widow Brown's, Owen asked himself, where should he go. He could not go far on the old horse and would be easily caught if pursued. His only hope lay in following the directions the rapparee had given.

Another hour must have gone by before he came to the wall overgrown with ivy. He passed an iron gate through which he could see the big house where Hugh was enjoying rest and refreshment. Suddenly Owen was shaking with anger. He heard again his cousin denying his native tongue. Though the Bourkes had come with the Norman French, they had intermarried with the proud O'Reillys and O'Briens. Hugh, as well as Owen, had grown up speaking the old language of the kings of Ireland.

Owen forced his thoughts away from Hugh's perfidy. He must keep his wits about him. When he came to the lane leading into the Widow Brown's cottage, the horse could not be held back. He turned in, with more speed than he had shown all day. He would have carried Owen right into the stable, had he not slid off the horse's back.

A little old woman with a black shawl wrapped around her head came out of the cottage.

"I've been expecting you," she said kindly, her eyes studying him shrewdly. "Come right in."

"I'll see to the horse first."

"That's good sense. But you look tired enough. I'll see to old Moll myself. Go sit down while I do."

Owen entered the clean little kitchen with its peat fire glowing on the hearth. The warmth felt good, for the chill of evening was in the air. He was stiff and sore, and dirty. He stood with his back to the fire until the widow returned. She looked him over before she said, "There's water and towels out in the shed. I'll have supper ready when you've cleaned up."

When Owen came back into the kitchen there was milk and lamb stew on the table. He ate and drank hungrily. When he finished, the widow, who had watched him with great satisfaction, asked, "Did you meet anyone on the road?"

"Yes, three horsemen on their way to Purcell's. They asked if I had seen a coach on the road. I had not, I told them."

"Sure they'd not brains enough to see the gentleman under the dirt," she said when he had finished. "But it's bad there being so near this night."

"I know. It's better I shouldn't stay."

"And where would you be going?"

Where indeed, Owen wondered.

"Now take yourself up to the loft. It'd not be the first time Tim Feenan has spent the night. Joe Gorman, the groom, will be down a bit later for a gossip I've no doubt. I'll find out what goes on up there," she jerked her head in the direction of the big house, "then we'll know where we're at. Now, up with you."

Owen was glad enough to lie down on the straw pallet in the loft. He listened for the groom's coming. To the murmur of voices below he fell asleep.

CHAPTER NINE

It seemed to Owen only a minute later when he was awakened by a poke in the ribs. Opening his eyes, as he moved away from the painful prodding, he saw that it was still dark.

"Are you awake, lad?" It was the Widow Brown's voice. "You'll have to come down now."

Owen groped for the brogans which he had taken off to relieve the soreness in his heel. Carrying them in one hand, he felt the other grasped by the widow's bony fingers. Cautiously he moved with her towards the opening where the ladder came up from the kitchen.

"Come down quietly," she said, as she dropped his hand.

In the kitchen the fire was out. As his eyes became accustomed to the gloom, Owen could make out the dim outlines of the windows and the shapes of table and settle.

"Sit down here, lad." A hand on his shoulder pushed

him into the one chair. He could feel rather than see that the woman sat down opposite him on the settle.

"I daren't have a fire or light a candle," she said. "For if any above saw it, it might set them to wondering. And it's bad news Joe brought me." She paused, sighing. "They'll be down in the morning to question Tim some more, he told me. If the master comes with them, he'll know you're not Tim. I could wish you were ten miles farther on your way."

"I'll have to leave at once then."

Owen's first thought was that Hugh had belatedly recognized his cousin in the boy on the road. He stood up.

"Sit down, lad. It's no good to panic. We must think what's to be done."

"You are right, of course." Owen sat down. He tried to be calm, but his mind raced along to the consequences of his being recognized. For if his presence in Ireland had been detected, his chances of recovering the Maryland documents had sharply declined. For even Hugh would know that Owen would not have left France except for some urgent reason. From there it would be an easy step to conclude that in the hurried flight of Owen and his mother, the precious papers had been left behind.

"Why is it they want to question Tim further? Yesterday they seemed satisfied that I knew nothing of the coach they were looking for."

"It was the English officer. He asked Joe would you be staying the night. He thought you might know more than that turncoat, who couldn't speak his own tongue, found out, Joe said."

Owen felt calmer. As long as his identity was not questioned, there was still a chance he might get away, a chance he must take.

"And why are they waiting until morning?" he asked next.

"The Englishman was for coming right down then and there, Joe said. But the other two were hungry and thirsty. When Joe assured them Tim always stayed the night and did a job of work for me to pay for the loan of the horse, the Englishman agreed to wait. And they'll not be too early, for they were still sitting over the wine when Joe left. But they'd best not find you when they do come. What's to do I don't know, for I was to keep you here for the day. One was to come for you after dark. But now I daren't let you stay. It would go hard with me if the Master knew I was helping my own."

"I'll not let that happen," he said stoutly. "You said a while back that you wished I was ten miles away. Why was that?"

"Sure you're a smart one." The widow's voice was more cheerful. "Ten miles farther on is Peter Fallon's farm. You'd be safe with him and he's the one would know how to let your friends know where you are. But how to get you there I don't know."

"Couldn't I walk, if you'd tell me the way."

"Could you, now?" Owen felt that she was looking at him sharply, though there was little she could see in the dark. "You were limping when you got off the horse last evening."

"The brogan cut into my heel," he explained. "If you

could give me something to wrap around it inside the stocking, it would help."

"I'll do better than that." He could hear her moving around now in the dark room. Soon she was putting a wet lump in his hand. "Put that against the sore and tie it on with this." He could feel the bandage's soft linen.

After removing his heavy woolen stocking, Owen placed the wet poultice against the blister, tying it securely with the linen strip. As he put on his stockings and shoes, he could feel the heat going out of the blister.

"Now that's fine," he said, standing up. "If you'll tell me the way to Peter's, I'll be off."

"You keep to the high road until you come to a strip of hazelwood, a good eight miles from here. Beyond the wood is a stream. Turn off the road there and follow the water south. Peter's will be the first house you come to. Tell him you're Tim Feenan, come from the Widow Brown's, and he'll understand. Here's a bit of bread and cheese to eat on the way. You'd better be starting now, for the dawn's coming."

Owen tried to thank her for what she had done, but she brushed his attempt aside. Then he asked, "What will you tell them, when they come looking for Tim in the morning?"

"The truth," the widow replied, as cheerful as a cricket, "that you left at dawn, though I'll not be above suggesting that it was back home you went, as your mother had need of you."

"And if they do go to Tim's house, will he tell them he's not been here at all?"

"Never fear that. Didn't he leave the horse for you to

bring back to me? He'll not give you away. Now you've nothing to fear unless the dogs that are minding the sheep set up a racket."

"I've chanced more than that to get this far." With a "God save you," from the widow, he stepped out into the night. Already it was beginning to lighten a little. A mist lay over the land, but it was not thick enough to shroud the outlines of house and barn, so he found his way out of the yard and onto the highway. Even in the dark he could make out the road, lighter than the fields that edged it. At least he was moving west again. If he could but cover the next ten miles, he would be safe. Let his cousin Hugh sleep in his soft bed. With every step Owen was closer to getting the Maryland grant. Hugh would be mad enough if ever he learned that he had looked at his cousin on the road without knowing him.

Owen heard a sheep dog bark, too far away to suggest that he was disturbed by someone passing on the road. Owen kept on and soon the barking ceased. The darkness lightened to gray, the mist changed to a soft rain. There would be no sun to warm him this day. Owen shivered in his damp clothing. It was a good thing, just the same, for the rain and the mist would screen him from any distant observer. Without the sun he had no idea of the time. When it seemed he must have walked halfway to the Fallon farm, he stopped by a brook to eat his bread and cheese, washing it down with the clear water. As he wiped off his face, he remembered how the rapparee had smeared it with dirt, and did the same so that his clean, untanned skin would not betray him.

When he felt as if his legs would carry him no farther,

he saw, a short way off, the hazelwood he had been looking for. Almost at the same moment, he heard, coming from behind him, the sound of galloping horses. Turning around, he saw that a bend in the road hid them. They must not see him, but he could not get to the wood in time. There were low furze bushes by the side of the road, with a ditch beyond. He quickly jumped over the bushes and lay down in the mud of the ditch. Just in time, for the sound of jingling harness was close. The horses were slowed to a walk, so that Owen feared he had been seen. He did not move and hardly breathed until they were well beyond his hiding place. As he lifted his head carefully to peer through the bushes, the horses broke into a run again. There were at least ten and the riders wore English uniforms. Soon he could hear them no longer. Getting back onto the road, he ran towards the hazelwood, though his brogans were sloshing and his clothing heavy with mud. Coming at last to the stream, he gladly turned off the highway. Stumbling and panting, he followed the brook through the woods. He was screened from the road by the trees, and the noise of water falling over stones was louder than his footsteps, even when fallen branches cracked under his weight.

The trees began to thin out and he could see ahead a whitewashed farmhouse. As he came near it, a dog ran barking from the farmyard, followed by a man who quickly suppressed the noise.

"I'm Tim Feenan," Owen managed to gasp.

"Be you now?" The man looked amused, but as Owen tried to say more, his arm was taken. "Come within lad. You look as if you'd had a bad time on the road."

120

Within the warm kitchen, assured that his host was Pete Fallon, Owen told of the troop of horses which had passed him on the road.

"That's not good," Pete said. "But how is it you've come today and alone from the Widow Brown's?"

Owen explained what the groom had said about the guests at the big house coming to question Tim. Pete gave a low whistle.

"It may be no accident that the soldiers are on the road, then. Could be they'll be coming here. I'd best hide you, though I'm sorry I can't let you dry out first. It's ten miles around by the road, but they could be here soon. Come with me."

Reluctantly Owen left the warm fire, following Pete out to the stable. There were no cattle or horses in the dim and dusty place. Up to the loft they went, Pete picking up a broom on the way. In the middle of the floor, he swept away the loose hay. Then he stepped on a spot where two of the rough boards had been sawed through. Their other ends rose in the air.

"Sit on the floor there and slide down under," he told Owen. As he did so, the boy felt a coarse wool blanket being handed to him.

"Pull it around you. It'll help to keep out the chill."

Pete replaced the boards and Owen could hear the swish of the broom pushing the hay back over them. He put his damp sleeve over his mouth and nose to keep out the dust that came through. Then he heard Pete's footsteps retreating across the loft and down the ladder. In spite of the blanket, Owen shivered in his damp clothes.

A long time passed before he heard the sound of horses' hooves and men's voices in the yard. Then there were footsteps inside the stable and on the ladder to the loft. Owen held his breath until he heard the searcher going down the ladder again and out of the stable. After several slowly passing minutes, he heard the creak of leather as the men mounted, then the sound of hooves moving away. Only then did he dare to move his cramped legs.

It seemed an hour before Owen heard footsteps enter the stable again. This time they came unhesitatingly up the ladder and across the loft floor. The boards above his head moved upward as Pete's voice said, "Reach for my hand, then stand up."

Owen did so, feeling he could not have stood without that supporting hand, so stiff was he from lying so long in the small space. In the complete darkness, for Pete carried no lantern, Owen was glad of the guiding arm which supported him, as they walked over to the ladder.

Back in the kitchen once more, Owen went to the hearth to warm himself.

"You can get out of those damp clothes, now," Pete said. "There's warm water for a bath and you can wrap this shawl around you when you're through. Hang your clothes on the crane so the fire can dry them."

Warm and clean again, with the shawl wrapped around him like a toga, Owen was soon sitting at the table eating the hot stew Pete served him.

"The English captain is thorough," Pete said. "He's had his men over every road and lane from here to Dublin. And never a sign of the coach they're looking for, or the man and boy that were in it. 'I guess it's sunk in the bog' one of the soldiers said, as they rode away.

Sure they'd have a better chance of finding it, if it were," Pete added with a smile.

Owen wondered how much this kind man knew. In his house Owen felt safe and protected, with no need to think of the morrow, which was as well, for he was very tired. He yawned when he had finished the heartening food.

"You can sleep easy tonight," Pete told him, "and as long into the morning as you've a mind to. For here you'll stay until tomorrow night."

He led Owen into an inner room, which held little more than the straw pallet where Owen stretched himself. Pulling a blanket over him, he hardly heard Pete close the door.

The next evening Owen sat again by the fire, dressed in the gray frieze suit which had been dried and brushed. When he had awakened from his long sleep, Pete had told him that someone would come for him that night, so he was not alarmed when there were two faint knocks on the door. Pete made no move until the knocks were repeated three times in quick succession then, after a pause, twice again. Owen recognized the rapparee's signal with a lift of his heart.

Through the door which Pete opened, in walked Sean O'Kelly. He looked at Owen as if he had never seen him before.

"Here's the lad, ready to go," Pete said. "But first you'll have a bite of supper." Sean nodded, taking a seat by the table. While Pete busied himself at the hearth,

Sean looked directly at Owen, a familiar glint of mischief in his blue eyes. Then he turned to take the bowl of stew Peter offered him, his face as solemn as a rapparee's should be.

Sean did not linger over his meal, though he ate heartily. Soon he led Owen out behind the stable where two garrons were tethered.

"Give your horse his head," Sean whispered as they mounted.

Owen could see nothing in the blackness under the trees, but his mount had no difficulty following Sean's. In a little while they came to the road, where the horses ran freely and Owen felt the wind in his face at last as they rode towards the west through the starless night.

CHAPTER TEN

Six days and many miles later, from the ridge of a hill at dawn, Owen and Sean saw the Shannon flowing south and west below them. For the first time on their ride across Ireland, Owen was looking at a familiar scene. Beyond the lower hills was Keeper Mountain, like the face of an old friend.

Turning expectantly to his companion, Owen was amazed at the black look he received from Sean. "What is it? Aren't you glad we're near the end of our road?"

"Glad enough." A brief smile lighted Sean's face. "I was but thinking this is the second time I've crossed this land, an outcast and a fugitive, where once it had belonged in all its length and breadth to my people."

During their days together Sean had told Owen how his family had traveled to Cork expecting to sail to France on the English ships. His father and brothers, all soldiers, had been given passage, but his mother was refused. His father had told Sean to stay with her. Like others whom Owen remembered seeing on the road, they had made their way back home.

"It will be ours again," Owen said confidently. "Had you seen the army as I did, ready to strike."

"Aye! It must have been a fine sight. May the day be soon when I'll see my father and brothers again! Now let's be on our way. We'll keep along this ridge until we are opposite the ford at Killaloe."

Within an hour they could see below them the yellow bank which marked the ford. Without pausing, Sean guided his horse down the slope and into the water. Following him, Owen felt the swift current against his legs and seeping through his heavy brogans. Though it was not the icy water of January, it was chilly enough to send a shiver up his back.

When they reached the opposite bank, Sean took the road through the wood behind the town. Owen had no need for a guide now. When they came onto the highway, the sun was warm on their backs. Sean urged his horse on so that they rode at a gallop until they came to the lane which led to the Cloona stables. Here he stopped.

"You'll not need me now, Owen. I'll ride on to let O'Cahane know we've come through safely."

"Thanks to you."

"It was your own quick wit saved us the night we slept in the field where the farmer found us at dawn. He'd have kept us to help with the ploughing. And him with soldiers quartered in his house. I'd never have thought up your story that they'd put us in the army if they saw us. I'll be on my way. We'll meet again before you leave."

Owen turned his horse into the woods that were part of the Bourke estate. Riding along he forgot about Sean, as he looked on the land he had lost. Anger at Hugh Bourke surged up, but he fought it. He was here now on a dangerous errand because it had mastered him on the winter's night when he, with his mother and Anna, had traveled this road away from Cloona. The sights and sounds and scents of home surrounded him. He was glad to be here, whatever the reason.

Where the lane ended behind the stable, he halted his horse and alighted. He stood a moment, uncertain as to the best way to let Patrick know of his arrival. Even as he did, he heard footsteps and Patrick saying, "No barking now, there's a good dog," followed by a muffled bark from Brian.

When they came to the corner of the stable, Patrick dropped the rope by which he had been holding Brian. In two leaps the dog was upon his master, his paws on the boy's chest, while from his throat came rumbles of joy.

"Hush, Brian, hush! We must keep still," Owen cried, resting his head against the soft fur of the dog's neck. Then pushing Brian away, he turned to Patrick who stood waiting.

"Master Owen! I've worried you all across Ireland. It's glad I am you're here at last." He held the boy in his arms for a moment, then stood off to look at him. "It's tired and hungry you must be. Come, for I've a bit of meat roasting in the pot."

Inside the cottage, Owen sat with Brian's head on his knee. Patrick busied himself about the hearth, stopping more than once to ask about his mistress and Captain Richard. His eyes glowed as Owen told of his visit to the camp near La Hogue.

"What a grand day it will be, when we see our men back in Limerick! But I've wondered more than once, Master Owen, since I heard you were coming secretly, how it was you weren't with your uncle, instead of in Ireland. I couldn't figure it out at all."

Owen felt his cheeks grow hot. For he must confess his foolish impulse to burn Cloona. How long ago and far away such childishness seemed! How could he tell Patrick of it! But there was no other way. He began by telling of the secret hiding place where the Maryland documents had been kept.

"I knew from your grandfather that he had the grant, but not where it was kept," Patrick said. "I always suspected that when your grandfather rebuilt the house he had a hiding hole somewhere, but where it was I did not know. It was as well, too, for Hugh suspicioned there was one and asked me about it. I could swear truthfully that I knew nothing about such a place."

"He looked for it? Do you think he found it?"

"That he didn't, for he told me he'd bring one who was expert in such matters when he returned. And he's not been back since."

"Then I'm on time." In his relief Owen realized how unsure he had been of finding the papers still there. "Though none too soon." He told Patrick of his meeting with Hugh in Kildare. "I had a bad moment. It's a good thing for me he isn't too bright."

"Sure he was never like the rest of the Bourkes," Patrick said. "Your father's line had the brains. But tell me the rest. For I don't understand how your mother would have gone off without those documents."

Shamefaced, Owen told of his part in that failure. At the end, Patrick patted the boy's knee, saying softly, "Sure it was natural enough. I wanted more than once to burn the place myself. Only the hope of the true Bourkes' return restrained me."

Patrick had heard no news of Father D'Arcy but had no doubt that O'Cahane had. "If he has, you'll be hearing it soon," Patrick promised. Then he left Owen by the fire while he went about his usual tasks in the stable.

When evening came, the two of them moved like shadows across the deserted yard to the kitchen door. Patrick carried a lantern, its flame carefully shielded so that no bobbing light might arouse the curiosity of travelers on the road.

Inside the kitchen it was very dark. Cautiously, Patrick uncovered the lantern, holding it so that no ray could shine through the bare windows. The light blinked back from the row of copper pans that hung by the fireplace.

"Let us get into the passage quickly," Owen whispered.

Hurrying across to the hearth, Owen opened the door beside it which led into the narrow hall. There were no windows here to send out a betraying gleam, so when Patrick had shut the door behind him, he let the lantern's light shine into the study beyond. Its shuttered windows prevented anyone outside from seeing into the room.

The air was musty. There was dust on the table and on the sheeting which had been flung over the chairs. Owen looked around in dismay. "Why hasn't Ellie kept this room clean, as she has the kitchen?"

"Hugh Bourke's orders were that no one was to go beyond the kitchen and no one has, until tonight. So let us get our task over, for I would not linger here." Patrick limped over to the fireplace.

Without hesitation Owen went to the bookshelves and, taking two books from the end of the third row, felt along the molding for the fourth notch. When the shelves swung back, he thought of how many times he had dreamed of doing this during the long months in Paris. He stepped into the darkness, followed by Patrick with the lantern. By its wavering light, the room looked just as it had when Owen had first seen it. Quickly he pulled out the lower drawer of the chest. The false bottom lifted and there the documents lay. Suddenly his knees felt weak. As he stood up, he grasped Patrick's arm for support. He had succeeded. Never, he vowed, would these documents fall into Hugh's hands. On an impulse he dropped to his knees to breathe a prayer of thanksgiving. Only when he stood up again did he realize that Patrick had stiffened to attention. Owen thought he could hear the faint sound of hoofbeats through the thick walls.

"The rapparees, I've no doubt," Patrick whispered. "But you'd best not be seen. I'll go out. I'll have to take the lantern, but I'll be back for you as soon as ever I can."

He went out closing the panel behind him. The darkness was complete. Pressing against the heavy cloth,

Owen listened tensely. At first he could hear nothing. Then gradually he became aware of myriad small sounds within the house: the wind in the chimney, the creaking of the unbolted panel, the scurrying of mice in the walls and across the stone floor.

He recalled his mother's determined battle against the field mice, which had sought to invade the house each fall. Since there was no longer anyone to oppose them, they had apparently taken possession. He thought sadly of how many things must be decaying now that his mother was no longer there. Hugh had shown little interest in the property he had taken from them, for he had stayed but a day in the winter, Patrick had said.

Patrick seemed to have been gone a long time, but Owen was not alarmed. Here in the very heart of Cloona, the enfolding walls were protection from whatever threatened. Then he heard the grating of the hinges and Patrick's lantern showed as the panel swung open.

"It was the rapparees, with O'Cahane himself. I told him you were here, though I've no doubt he already knew it. He wants to see you. Tomorrow you're to ride to the cave. Now, if you have the papers, we'll be off."

"Patrick, I'm thinking of the vestments and altar vessels. Surely we ought not to leave them for Hugh to find."

"If we could get them to Limerick, I've no doubt the good fathers would be glad of them. Maybe a way can be found. Meanwhile they'd best stay here, for there's no safe place in the cottage to hide them. Come now."

Owen went with him, clutching the precious documents in his hands. As they came into the kitchen, Patrick extinguished the lantern, for white moonlight poured in through the windows. Before they left the shelter of the doorway, he said in a low voice, "Try to keep in my shadow as we cross the yard so it will look as if only one was walking here."

Owen obeyed, but he was glad when they had reached the cottage and, safe behind its shuttered windows, he could move more freely.

"Had O'Cahane any news of Father D'Arcy?" he asked.

Patrick shook his head.

"What news did he bring, Patrick?"

"Sit down, lad." Patrick threw another clump of turf on the fire. "It's bad news he brought. The French fleet has been defeated. There are no ships to transport the army."

"Oh, no!" It was a cry of pain. "But if the army is still intact, mightn't it be that another fleet will be assembled?"

"That I wouldn't know. But let's think of what's to do now. We'd best find a way to hide your papers safely until O'Cahane finds a way to send you back to France. I've no doubt it's about that he wants to see you."

Owen could think of nothing but the French fleet swinging proudly at anchor as he had seen it only a few weeks ago.

"Come lad. No use to sit and mourn. It's all the more important that these documents be in a safe place."

"I know. Why not inside the lining of my coat? That's where I planned to carry them before. Could you manage a needle and thread to sew it back if we ripped it?"

"That I can, well enough. But I'm wondering if under

one of the floor boards might not be better, until you're ready to leave. It's a big responsibility for you to carry them always."

"But, Patrick, I might have to leave in a hurry, or it could be that I might be off somewhere and could not return." Owen shook his head. "That would be risking too much."

"You're right, lad. Give your coat here and I'll show you how I learned to sew in the army."

Owen sat at the other end of the settle and watched Patrick bent over his task. The firelight glowed on the grizzled head, highlighting the few red hairs left among the gray; lighting up the strong features which had grown heavy with the years; marking the lines that grief had etched on the face which Owen recalled as always merry, until the day Patrick had returned to Cloona with the news that his master had fallen at the Boyne.

Remembering the sorrow of that far-off day, Owen thought that maybe Patrick would be the only one left of those who had filled his childhood with joy and affection. His mother was in England where he dared not go. Uncle Richard might fall on the battlefield before King James was restored to his throne.

"When I go this time, won't you come with me, Patrick? You can't want to stay here with Hugh Bourke for your master?"

"That I don't and won't." Patrick looked deep into the fire, as if to read the future there. "But what would I do in a strange country? You've no need of me there and I'd only be a care to you."

"But I shall need you, Patrick. Until I finish school, as

I promised Mother I would, Monsieur Castillon would find a place for you I'm sure. I wager that in all of France there's not a better man with horses. Then," Owen forced himself to look into the possible future, "if the army does not return, I'd want to go to Maryland. I'd need you then."

"I'd not want your father's son to set out for the colonies without me. I could be of use to you there. We'll talk more about it another time, Master Owen." Patrick's voice was cheerful. "You'll be wanting some sleep now."

Willingly Owen climbed the ladder to the loft where he was to spend the night. Though Patrick had wanted to give up his bed, Owen thought it more prudent to make no change in Patrick's normal living arrangements. The cramped space under the roof was luxury after the nights spent in the open. Owen could not restrain a bitter thought of his room in the house across the courtyard. Would he ever sleep there again?

When he awoke to daylight, Owen could not tell whether it was early or late. The only sound he could hear from below was an occasional hiss from the turf burning on the hearth. Nonetheless he moved cautiously over to the opening where he could see there was no one in the room below. Upon climbing down, he found a pitcher and basin for his use. A pan of stirabout was warming by the hearth. He was hungry. After a quick splashing of cold water on his face, he sat down to eat, wondering what hour it was, where Patrick could be, and if it would be safe to step out the door.

All of his questions were answered when Patrick appeared in the doorway. "So you waked at last. It's well

towards noon, lad, You must have been weary indeed."
He came into the room to sit down beside Owen. "You'd
best be starting for O'Cahane's cave when you're
through. You remember the way and the signal?"

"Indeed, yes." Owen would never forget them.

"Take the track that runs back of the village. Should
you pass anyone, you must not greet him, for that is the
way of the rapparees, as you know. It will be well if you
are mistaken for one of them."

Patrick went towards the door. There he stood, his
hands on the frame, his face raised, as if he had stepped
out to look at the sky. Sensing that someone was about,
Owen waited quietly. When Patrick started forward, as
quickly as his limp would allow, Owen kept close by his
side.

"It was only Ellie going to her cottage," Patrick explained when they entered the stable. "If you stay here,
she'll have to know, I'm thinking, but we'll wait a bit
before telling her."

Owen rode Sheelah out the back way and turned toward the west. How often he had galloped along this lane
on Donegal, with Brian running at the horse's hooves.
But Donegal was gone from the stable, and Owen realized Brian had not been around this morning.

Sheelah ran swiftly along the rutted way. Through the
trees Owen could see the gray clouds scudding eastward.
It would rain before night. Coming to the main road he
halted Sheelah, looking carefully in each direction before
turning. The road was as deserted as it had been on the
gray January day he had last ridden this way, but how
different the land looked. Then it had been all gray and

brown. Today, even in the sunless light, there was spring color everywhere: golden furse in the bogland, leaves in every shade of green in the woods, bright blossoms by the roadside.

Owen was relieved when he came to the track across the bog, having met no one since he left Cloona. When he entered the wood, he was met by one of the rapparees, who silently took the horse's reins and gestured Owen towards the cave. Within its lighted chamber O'Cahane was seated at the table. Getting up, he extended his hand to Owen.

"So you're here and safe for a while, lad."

"Thanks to you for sending Sean. I'd never have found my way without him."

"You made the worst ten miles by yourself, don't forget."

Owen was too surprised to reply to this praise. But O'Cahane continued, "You've grown up a lot since the night I carried you over the threshold of Cloona. I know that my haste then is what has brought you back into danger, so I'll see you out of it. I sent for you to make plans for getting you off to France, but there is one whose need is more urgent."

"Is it Father D'Arcy?" Owen asked.

"Yes." O'Cahane sat silently, while Owen waited impatiently for news of his friend.

When O'Cahane began to speak, the words came slowly, almost reluctantly. "Father is near here now, with English soldiers on his trail. I must find a place to conceal him and I would rather it would not be here."

Owen guessed that, like Patrick, O'Cahane suspected

that there was a "hiding hole" at Cloona and waited for Owen to confirm that suspicion. He did not hesitate. The time was past for the hidden room to be kept a secret.

"There's a place at Cloona where I'm sure he would be safe."

"Even if the house were searched?"

"Hugh could not find it, and he tried. When will Father get here? Shall I wait to take him back with me?" In his eagerness Owen forgot that, in O'Cahane's presence, he was supposed to answer questions, not ask them.

But he was not reproved for his boldness, as O'Cahane asked: "Does Patrick know this place?"

"I showed it to him last evening."

"Good! I'll have the priest taken directly there. He is nearer Cloona than here. It will take but a moment to arrange. Wait." He went quickly to the cave entrance and Owen heard the shrill curlew's call, summoning one of the rapparees. Left alone, he wondered where Father D'Arcy had been since the coach had lumbered off along the lane in Kildare.

"What danger threatens Father now?" Owen asked when O'Cahane returned.

"He's a hunted man," was the reply. "A priest who dares to come into this country is an enemy to the English. Now that the army will not return, those who have been waiting to pick the winning side will go over to William, ready to betray their own. Much good will it do them." Owen caught the threatening note in the man's voice and remembered tales of the rapparees' vengeance.

"Patrick told me that the fleet had been destroyed. It

is hard for me to believe, for I saw the great ships riding at anchor waiting for others, to transport the army."

"King James grew weary of 'the Protestant wind' that kept the Mediterranean fleet from joining Tourville's and ordered it out. He had been assured that at least some of the English ships would come over to him when he showed his strength." O'Cahane's face grew red with anger. "He risked all on the word of the English and he has lost. The French ships were driven onto the beaches and burned." He slumped wearily in his chair.

Owen said, "But surely King Louis will give him another fleet?"

O'Cahane jumped to his feet. "Don't talk nonsense," he shouted. "You're only a boy, but you should know better. How long has Ireland put her faith in the false Stuarts and looked for help from the French king? When the army was here, willing to fight and die to the last man, if need be, did Louis send the guns which might have saved us? No! No!"

"You think it hopeless, then?" Owen asked timidly, for O'Cahane seemed to be waiting for some response.

"Hopeless? Has it ever been anything else? When all the fighting men left the country to the mercy of its conquerors, what hope was there that they would return? I tell you they were all traitors who sailed with Sarsfield. All of them."

How dare this man call Uncle Richard a traitor? Owen looked straight into the blazing eyes across the table. Then he clamped his teeth to hold back the angry words that stormed inside him. This man was his friend and protector. Owen forced himself to stay calm, knowing that Father D'Arcy's safety and his own might depend on it.

O'Cahane appeared poised for an indignant retort. When it did not come, he said brusquely, as if he too were struggling for control, "You'd better go now. The priest will reach Cloona ahead of you." He laid his hand on Owen's shoulder, as if to push him out of the cave.

Owen ran down the hill to mount Sheelah and was hardly aware of the rapparee who handed him the reins. Anger boiled inside of him so that he was halfway out to the road before he knew that it was raining, a thin drizzle that penetrated his clothing and cooled his burning face.

CHAPTER ELEVEN

Owen halted Sheelah at the end of the track, looking carefully in both directions before taking the road towards Cloona. As far as he could see, the land lay quiet under the rain. He gave Sheelah her head and she ran towards home, as eager for shelter as he was to see Father D'Arcy. For had not O'Cahane said that the priest would be at Cloona first.

When they came to the lane which went back of the village, Owen had to restrain Sheelah. Having made certain that they were unobserved, he turned in, still keeping a tight rein. At the first bend another horse and rider blocked their path. The gray frieze of the rider and the unkempt garron were reassuring; but wise in the ways of the rapparees, Owen halted and sat quietly waiting for the man to speak. Beckoning Owen to follow, the rapparee rode in among the trees. When they were well hidden, he brought his mount close to Sheelah. In a low voice he said, "The priest is now at Cloona. His pursuers are close behind. If possible, they will be delayed until you can join him. You must wait by the tall oak just out of sight of the stable. You know it?"

Owen nodded, as eager as Sheelah to be on the way.

"Tether your horse well off the path. Stay close enough yourself to see anyone coming, but not to be seen. Wait there for someone to come to tell you all is well, or until you hear the signal. If the latter, you must ride back to the cave."

Without another word he was gone. Of her own accord Sheelah turned back to the track. She would have galloped if Owen had not held her in. On the long road across Ireland, he had learned from Sean that it was foolhardy to go at that pace, not knowing what lay ahead. Better the slow silent run to which he held her, anxious though he was to get to Cloona and Father D'Arcy. Owen was hungry, his clothes were damp from the steadily falling rain, and he did not want to ride again to the cave to face O'Cahane.

When he came to the oak tree, he turned Sheelah into the woods, though she fought to continue on to the stable. The trees were so close together that he had to dismount and lead the horse by the bridle until he came to a little clearing. Having tethered Sheelah to a stout branch, he walked back to the oak tree, hoping that someone would come for him soon. Squatting down behind some bushes, he could see for some distance. He was far from comfortable and knew he must find some other way of keeping under cover if he had long to wait.

He thought how fortunate it was that he had shown the secret room to Patrick. Father D'Arcy would be safe there, he felt sure. Then he saw Patrick coming, his limping gait unmistakable. Crashing out of the bushes, Owen ran to meet him.

"Thanks be to God you're here lad! The searchers have not reached Cloona yet, but there's not a moment to be lost. Where is Sheelah?"

"I'll get her." Owen hurried through the trees to where the horse was tied. She nickered eagerly as he unfastened her and led her to where Patrick waited.

"You ride, Patrick." Owen handed over the reins. "Then you can tell me what has happened."

Patrick mounted willingly, for he was still out of breath. Sheelah was ready to run home, but he held her in so that Owen could walk beside him.

"You'd hardly been gone an hour when two rapparees came riding in with Father D'Arcy. They brought instructions from O'Cahane that I was to hide him in the place only you and I knew."

"How glad I am you knew it, Patrick."

"Yes, he's tucked away there. The rapparees are watching, so it will be safe for you to go in. But you'd best go directly while I stable Sheelah. Then, if I can, I'll bring you some dry things to put on."

While Patrick talked, they had come to the clearing back of his cottage. They waited for a moment, listening. There was no sound but the soft dripping of the rain.

"Go quickly, now, Master Owen. When you get into the room, push the bolt. Do not release it until I come. I will knock twice, then three times, the rapparees' signal. Wait until I repeat it."

Owen grasped Patrick's hand for a moment, then moved off to the right of the cottage. It was quiet enough as he came into the courtyard and crossed to the kitchen. As the heavy door shut behind him, he heard the curlew's call. Three times the whistle was repeated while he listened, his heart beating rapidly. Then the two answering notes sounded, so close, they seemed to come from just outside the door.

The half-light of dusk coming in the windows was enough for him to see his way across the kitchen and down the passage to the study. There he had to feel his way across to the bookshelves beside the fireplace. When he had removed the two books, he pressed against the panel. As it moved inwards, he replaced them.

A single candle burned on the chest. Carefully Owen swung the panel back into place and bolted it before turning to the priest, who rose from the cot where he had been lying.

"Father!"

"Owen, my boy!" His arms embraced Owen. "I feared you might not get here on time. How glad I am you did!"

"And not a moment too soon, I'm thinking," Owen said as they sat together on the cot. "For I heard the rapparees' signal as I closed the kitchen door. Your pursuers must be near. But we'll be safe here, Father."

"I believe we will be, lad. Your grandfather built well. If I had not been assured there was, under this roof, a secure hiding place, I would not have come, bringing danger to you and to Patrick. But your clothes are damp, Owen. You must be cold and hungry. There is food on the chest. Eat now, for I think we should soon put out the candle."

Owen went over to the chest, where there was a pitcher

of milk, bread, and cheese. "Once I would have been sure that there wasn't a chink through which the light could be seen. But now that the mice have the run of the place, that may not be so."

Owen ate hastily, then gulped a mug of milk. Looking around, he saw that Patrick had brought blankets as well as food. He handed one to Father D'Arcy and laid the other on the floor near the cot. "This will be my bed. Now I'll count my steps over to the chest, so I can make my way back in the dark. For it will be black indeed. I'm happy that my old home offers you protection and shelter this night."

"Thank you, Owen. I hope some day I may visit it under happier circumstances, but I'm grateful for the haven now."

"I think I'd better blow out the candle." Counting three footsteps, Owen walked to the chest and extinguished the light. Even as he did so, he heard faint sounds that might have been horses' hooves on the stone-paved yard. Turning, he took three careful steps, then felt the blanket under his feet.

"I'm back again," he whispered, feeling his way to the cot. "I think they've come. Can you hear anything?" In silence they waited, hearing only their own breathing. They heard a door slam then and footsteps so muffled by the thick walls that the intruders' movements were hard to follow. Owen tried to guess where they were. The soldiers, of course, were systematically searching the house. Anger flared in him as he pictured them going from room to room, investigating every corner, doubtless pounding the walls to find a hollow one. They must suspect that there was a hidden room, for they were common enough in the houses of Catholics in England as well as in Ireland. Although Owen did not understand how, he knew that this one had been contrived to defy the ordinary searcher.

Owen felt Father D'Arcy's breath on his face as whispered words sounded in his ear, "I think we should try to rest. I feel secure enough to sleep, even with enemies so close."

"They'll never find us," Owen replied before getting up from the cot. After rolling himself in the blanket, he lay on the stone floor, wondering if he could possibly sleep.

All was quiet. The tramping feet were still. Where were the soldiers now, Owen wondered. They were probably consulting about what to do next. He had heard tales of Elizabethan times when thwarted searchers had burned down houses in which they suspected a priest might be hiding. It could be done again. The thought gave him a few moments of horror. But it was unlikely that Cloona would be put to the torch, since it virtually belonged to Hugh Bourke. Even that bitter fact might serve some purpose. For if Owen and his mother had still been in possession, the house might well be destroyed, as had its predecessor in Cromwell's time.

Out of a confused dream where Hugh Bourke had been standing over him, Owen was suddenly wide awake. He was hot and the smell of smoke was in his nostrils. He had been wrong in assuming that the soldiers would not burn Hugh's property. He tugged at the blanket on the cot. Father D'Arcy's hand seized his and drew him close.

"What is it, Owen?"

"The heat!" Owen had difficulty in keeping his voice to a whisper. I'm afraid they're trying to burn us out."

Owen sensed that Father D'Arcy was sitting up. After a minute he spoke in a voice so low that it could barely be heard. "I think they have only built a fire to warm themselves. Do not be alarmed. I am confident no harm will come to us here."

Owen listened tensely. There was no sound of crackling flames, no increase in the heat that had frightened him. Father was right. The house was not burning down around them. His panic subsided and he lay down again. Soon he was asleep.

When Owen woke up, he felt that it was daytime, although no light came into the room to tell him so. He wondered if the soldiers were still in the house. He listened, but he could hear nothing except his companion's rhythmic breathing. His back and legs ached from pressing against the unyielding stone. If only he could stand up without wakening Father D'Arcy. Deciding to chance it, he began quietly to disentangle himself from the blanket. Before he had succeeded, there were two sharp raps on the wall. As he got to his feet, three more followed. Feeling his way to the panel, he reached for the bolt. With his fingers on it, he waited for the signal to be repeated, then pushed the bolt over. He had to jump back as the panel swung in and Patrick stepped through the opening, a lighted candle in his hand.

"They have gone?" Owen asked eagerly.

"Aye, lad!" Patrick's face lighted with a smile. "They're well on the road to Ennis now, watched every foot of the way by the rapparees. The danger has passed, praise be to God."

Owen turned to Father D'Arcy, who had awakened and was sitting on the side of the cot.

"And what hour of the day is it, Patrick?" the priest asked. "I might have slept a week, so rested am I."

" 'Tis well toward the middle of the morning, Father. And did you sleep the night through?"

"I did, though it's more than you did, I'm sure."

"And how could I sleep not knowing what was going on here? What a relief when they finally rode off this morning! 'There's no priest hiding here,' one said as they mounted their horses, 'so we'll ride towards Ennis. He must have gone that way.' And a good breakfast they had before they left, convinced I was an obliging fellow, though none too bright." Patrick chuckled. "And there's breakfast waiting for you, should you be hungry."

"I'm starving, Patrick," Owen said. "Let's get out of here."

"Is it safe for us both to appear in the daylight?" Father D'Arcy asked.

"There's no danger at all," Patrick replied. "For there are rapparees on guard on all sides, though you'd never see them. There's none but them within a mile. They made sure of that. So come now."

Eagerly Owen and Father D'Arcy followed Patrick out into the daylight, blinking their eyes against the brightness and breathing the fresh, warm air with delight.

CHAPTER TWELVE

Later that day, Father D'Arcy, Patrick, and Owen sat on the grass beside the house, enjoying the sun. With the rapparees on guard, they had no fear.

"It is hard to realize that we cannot stay here forever," Owen remarked.

"You couldn't be safer, now that the soldiers have searched the place," Patrick said. "I hope, Father, you'll stay a while. 'Tis a bit of rest you need."

"Thank you, Patrick. Sitting here with this quiet scene before us, I might well feel that I could remain for a time. But we have only to remember last night to know how insecure we are. I must not delude myself. My presence places not only you but my good friends, the rapparees, in danger. Besides I have work to do."

"But, Father!" Owen exclaimed. "You said you'd had no sleep the night before last. I'm sure that's not the only time since I left you. Surely you'll stay for a day or two."

Father D'Arcy shook his head. "No, Owen, I must be off again as soon as I can arrange it."

"You're not thinking of going to Limerick?" Patrick asked. "That would be foolhardy, both for yourself and your friends."

"You're right, Patrick. I was not thinking of Limerick, but of Dublin."

"Not Dublin! Surely you're not going back there?"

Father D'Arcy laid his hand on Owen's shoulder. "I have a feeling Dublin might be a good place to be while the English hunt me in the west. If I could get there quickly, I might be able to finish my mission in that city, while the search goes on here. Don't you think so, Patrick?"

"You're probably right, Father." Patrick's answer was reluctant. "Though I'd like to see you stay here for a bit. When would you want to be leaving?"

"Tonight, if possible."

"Oh, not so soon," Owen begged.

"I'm sorry, Owen, but I feel it is best."

Patrick stood up. "If that is your wish, Father, I'll go to arrange it." He walked off towards the woods.

Owen watched Patrick until he was out of sight. Then he turned to the priest. "Will you take me to Dublin with you?"

"No, Owen. It would be better for you to stay here."

"But—" Owen began, then stopped in obedience to Father D'Arcy's upraised hand.

"I wish I could, Owen, but you would be risking too much, all that you returned to Ireland for. Our disguise as Mynheer van der Groate and his son, when we were in Dublin before, served my purpose as well as yours. Since that became suspect, the two of us in any disguise could attract attention dangerous to those I must see, as well as to us. Rome has sent me to visit as many as possible of the priests left in Ireland. I bring them instructions from the Holy See, from which they are cut off by the enemy fleet. My work will not be finished until I have done this and reported to Rome. We both will be safer if we part company here."

With that answer Owen had to be content, as Patrick returned. "You must ride to the cave, lad," he said. "The rapparees on guard cannot leave their posts and it will be late afternoon before they are replaced."

Owen got up reluctantly to walk towards the stables. He had hoped to have the rest of the day with Father D'Arcy. He sighed so audibly that Father D'Arcy, walking beside him asked, "What's troubling you, Owen?"

"I hate to leave you, when our time together is so short, Father. Then, I'm not anxious to see O'Cahane." He went on to tell of the rapparee leader's outburst and his own difficulty in holding back an angry reply.

"I'm proud of you, Owen. You've come a long way since you left Cloona in the autumn. I've no doubt O'Cahane thought so, too, when he calmed down. You need have no hesitancy in going to him. He's the one who should feel uncomfortable. But I see Patrick has your horse ready. Go quickly, so that you may the sooner return."

"That I'll do," Owen replied, mounting Sheelah and riding off.

Owen's shadow was long on the road as he rode back

to Cloona with a lighter heart. This was partly because today he could ride at ease, not watching every turn in the road, as he had yesterday. For O'Cahane had said that the way was guarded by the rapparees and would continue to be until Father D'Arcy left for Dublin. Even that parting was made less painful by the kindness of the rapparee leader, for he had astonished Owen by saying, "I'm sorry Father is not taking you with him. When I knew that you had returned to Ireland with him, I feared you would be a hindrance. Now I know you could be a help."

Those words had made Owen feel proud and strong. He had not thought it possible for O'Cahane to unbend as he had. Had he not asked pardon for his outburst of the day before and complimented Owen on his restraint in the face of such provocation. "Believe me, lad, I had forgotten about your uncle in my anger," O'Cahane had said. "Perhaps he and the thousands of other brave men who left Ireland were right and I am wrong."

Then that rare smile had flashed across his face as he took Owen's hand in his.

When Owen had spoken of the altar vessels and vestments still hidden at Cloona, O'Cahane had promised they would be sent to Limerick that night.

On the cart track now, Owen took a deep breath of the warm summer air, as Sheelah ran swiftly towards home. It was good to be here, he thought, with O'Cahane's assurance that he should stay with Patrick as long as it was safe, perhaps until passage to France could be arranged. "And that will be soon, I hope," the rapparee leader had said. "In spite of what I said yesterday, Ireland is no place for you, with your cousin Hugh eager to get control of you and the Maryland property, as well."

"Shall I see Sean again?" Owen had asked, and with the assurance that he would, he had ridden off.

When he reached Cloona, Owen found, to his disappointment, that Father D'Arcy was sleeping.

"I insisted on it," Patrick said. "There will be no rest for him tonight. What time will his escort come?"

"About an hour after sundown, O'Cahane said."

"Then we'll let the man rest until the sun sets, which will leave time for a bite and a word of farewell."

While they were talking, Owen had dismounted and led Sheelah into the stable. As Patrick was removing saddle and bridle, Owen wondered what he would do until sunset, perhaps two hours away. Maybe a romp with Brian—but where was the dog? In the comings and goings of the last two days, Owen had not missed him. He had been tied by the stable when Owen and Patrick had gone into the house two nights ago. Owen had not seen the dog since and asked Patrick, "Where is Brian?"

"Sure I forgot to tell you, what with Father's coming and all. Though I miss the dog myself, and will more after you've gone."

"But where is he, Patrick?"

"Now don't be alarmed, Master Owen. No harm has come to him. It's only that O'Cahane took him away the other night, lest he betray your presence to them who had better not know of it."

Though he could not condemn O'Cahane's carefulness, Owen was depressed about its restrictions. How quiet it was! He remembered the cheerful hum of activity from offices, yard, and stable in the days before his father had led his men off to war. Many, like him, had died in battle; others had gone to France; and the few left in the village came no more to Cloona. Owen wondered if Hugh would bring them back to till the fields, for the defeat of the French fleet meant that he would be master of Cloona now.

"Patrick, I think I'll take a look through the house while I can."

"That's a good idea, Master Owen."

Owen knew that Patrick's encouragement was given to keep him occupied while Father D'Arcy slept. Crossing the courtyard towards the kitchen door, Owen wished he had not spoken so impulsively. As suddenly as it had come, the desire to walk again through the familiar rooms of home had died. He would feel silly to turn away now, and so he opened the kitchen door. There was no fire on the hearth, no smell of good cooking in the air. Otherwise the room was little changed. Ellie had kept the copper pots shined and the deal table scrubbed white. He went through the pantries into the dining room. Though he knew Ellie's care had not extended beyond the kitchen, he was dismayed at what he saw. His mother's cherished mahogany was filmed with dust, the window panes were streaked from the frequent rains, and cobwebs hung from the ceiling.

Going into the hall and starting up the stairs, he recalled the last time he had been on that stairway, intent on burning the place. His face grew hot with shame as he saw himself flung over O'Cahane's shoulder to be carried from the house.

Shaking off the memory, Owen continued on his way. On the landing he turned towards the room that had been his as long as he could remember. Dust motes were thick in the shaft of sunlight coming through the western windows. A sheet had been flung across the unmade bed; the clothespress was empty and the mantel bare. He went quickly across the hall to his mother's room. Here, too, all the personal things had been taken away. He walked across the floor to fling open the dressing room door. Here all his clothes and his mother's had been dropped on tables, chairs, and floor. One pile had knocked over the inlaid box which had held sewing materials. On the floor nearby he saw the gold thimble which had been his father's first gift to his mother. He stooped to pick it up. She would be glad to have it. A whiff of lavender from her gowns brought his mother's presence back.

Dropping the thimble into his pocket, he rushed from the room, down the stairs, through hall and kitchen, and into the fresh air. Seeing Father D'Arcy at the door of the cottage, he went over to him.

"I have slept well, Owen. What word from O'Cahane? When do I leave?"

"The rapparees will come for you an hour after sunset." Owen glanced up to see the sun low in the sky. Father's time at Cloona was almost over. The shadow of his leaving, like those of the lengthening day, lay across the scene. Owen could no longer remember the things he had been longing to say last night when silence had been enforced by the soldiers' presence.

"Patrick will be wanting to know that you're awake,

Father." Owen turned towards the stable, where he met Patrick at the door.

"I see Father is awake. I'd best be getting him a bite to eat." He walked towards the cottage, Owen following.

Much later, Patrick and Owen were sitting on the cottage step, waiting for O'Cahane.

"It must be nearly midnight," Owen was saying when O'Cahane and two companions rode in. Owen and Patrick stood up as O'Cahane dismounted.

"We must work quickly. My men should be in Limerick before dawn."

Patrick went into the cottage and returned with the lighted lantern and the two saddlebags he had earlier taken from the stable.

"Be quick about it," O'Cahane said, sitting down on the step, as Patrick handed the lantern to Owen.

"Won't you come with us to see the hidden room?" Owen asked O'Cahane.

"But it is a family secret . . ."

"It will not be for long, I'm thinking," Owen replied. "Hugh is bound to find it. You might like to see it before he does."

"I would, indeed. I have guessed that there was a 'hiding hole' in the house, but I never could figure out where; and I knew the house well. Let us go."

"No more than two are needed," Patrick said, handing the saddlebags to O'Cahane. "I'll wait here."

As they walked across the courtyard, O'Cahane said, "You looked surprised, Owen, that I knew the house. I told you once that your grandfather acted for me with the Court of Claims to have restored to me my father's estate, for I was an orphan. It was no fault of his that I'm now an outlaw. Ah, well! If he had succeeded, I'd be landless again and in France with Sarsfield, I suppose."

By this time they had passed through the kitchen and into the study. "Aye," O'Cahane went on, "this is the room where I often sat while the Owen Bourke for whom you are named, lad, went over the papers of my claim. But that was all a long time ago."

Owen, meanwhile, had walked over to the fireplace and swung in the bookcase beside it.

"So that's where it is," O'Cahane exclaimed, still standing in the middle of the room. He followed Owen into the hiding place. Taking the lantern, he directed its beam around the walls. "Why it must be part of the old place that was burned in Cromwell's time!"

"All that was left when Grandfather returned from exile."

"And a clever man planned it." O'Cahane shifted the lantern around to see the whole of it. "But I must not waste time. Here are your treasures no doubt." He walked over to the chest.

"Yes." Owen came to his side and pulled open the top drawer. The lantern's light was reflected softly from the golden altar vessels. Reverently Owen took them out and wrapped them in the black cloth which had lain beneath them. With O'Cahane's help, he packed them in one of the bags. From the lower drawer they took the embroidered vestments. Folded carefully inside the linen surplice, they were placed in the other bag. Then Owen showed O'Cahane the false bottom where the Maryland grant had been kept.

Closing the drawer, Owen took a last look around. The blankets were still on the cot and the candlestick on the chest. He must remind Patrick to remove them in the morning.

They stepped out into the study and Owen once more swung the panel into place, showing O'Cahane the notched groove where the spring was pressed.

"Thank you, Owen, for sharing this secret. If you return to Cloona, it will be as if I never knew it."

When they came into the courtyard, Patrick took the bag from Owen and followed O'Cahane to where the two horsemen waited.

Owen snuffed out the lantern, then sat on the step thinking about what he had just done. He realized that his impulse to share the Cloona secret with O'Cahane sprang from a feeling, not before acknowledged, that he would not be returning. Lifting his head, he looked over at the gray walls of his home. The papers inside his coat moved with his movement. They represented a grant of land in Maryland, more land than remained in the shrunken Cloona estate. He could, had he but the strength and endurance, build a new home in that far place.

The two horsemen passed before the gray wall he had been staring at, as they rode out of the yard. O'Cahane, leading his horse, walked towards the cottage with Patrick.

When O'Cahane spoke, his voice was gentler than Owen had ever heard it. "It's been a good night's work,

Owen. You may be happy that your treasures are on the way to Limerick. A good thing too that Father D'Arcy is well on his way across Ireland. For I have learned that Hugh Bourke is in Limerick. He may be here tomorrow."

"So soon! Then do I go with you tonight?"

"No, Owen. You may stay with Patrick until tomorrow. I'll expect you early in the morning." After a slight pressure of his hand on Owen's shoulder, he mounted his horse and rode off.

Owen turned to Patrick. "Only this morning it seemed as if we might stay here forever."

"There's no safety for you in Ireland, Master Owen, with that rogue on the loose." Patrick sighed. "And there's worse I have to tell you. The French King has split up the Irish Army. It's no longer encamped on the cliffs across from England. Regiments are being scattered to fight with the French against the Dutch, the German Princes, and all Louis' enemies, who are too numerous to count."

Owen thought of that proud army he had seen so short a time ago. Now the Stuart king would never lead it back in triumph. "And Uncle Richard . . . What if he goes to Paris and I'm not there? I may be too late to see him when I get there, if I ever do."

"Now don't be worrying, Master Owen. You'll get there all right. O'Cahane will see to that. As for Captain Richard, you'll see him, I've no doubt. He will find a way."

Owen laid his hand on Patrick's gnarled fingers. "You'll not stay here, now," he pleaded. "You said before you'd think about coming to France with me. Surely you will now, when you know that if you stay, Hugh will be your master for always."

"I haven't forgotten. God willing, I'll be with you when you sail for France. For the present I stay here. I can be useful to others besides Hugh. Now, you'd best get some sleep."

CHAPTER THIRTEEN

The bright sunlight, the song of birds, and the scent of heather were carried on the warm breeze as Owen turned Sheelah into the track across the bog. The day was made for gladness, yet he was sad. For the last time, he thought, and the horse's hooves beat out the refrain—for the last time.

He stopped under the first trees. Dismounting, he gave the signal. The whistle sounded piercingly shrill in the quiet air. In a moment a rapparee stood beside him, seeming as usual to come out of the ground. With a final pat on Sheelah's sturdy, short neck, Owen turned to climb to the cave's entrance. When he came to the turn in the rocky wall where he could look into the lighted cave, he stood still. O'Cahane sat at the table, his head resting on his hands. Owen was pleased that he had come so quietly that no sound had alerted the rapparee leader. It was only when Owen moved into the lantern's light that O'Cahane raised his head.

"Come, sit down, lad." He motioned to the chair

across the table from him. "It's a sad morning for us, even though the sun shines."

"I couldn't believe it would happen, though you predicted it."

O'Cahane came around to sit on the table near Owen. "And if I did, I only half believed it. For since the news came, I've been able to think of nothing else. For this is the end. There'll be no more organized resistance. Ireland is England's now. There are no leaders left to dispute the claim. And what good if we had?" He seemed to be talking more to himself than to Owen. "Haven't we had the best for the past hundred years. O'Neill and O'Donnell, Owen Roe and Sarsfield, and hasn't it all ended in defeat?" He stood up and walked around the table, to fling himself into his chair.

"But this isn't settling your problems, Owen. Perhaps you'd like to know where you'll be sleeping and eating while you're waiting for a ship to take you to France?"

"I hope the waiting won't be long, for I know I'm a danger to you."

"Think nothing of that. My men and I have lived with danger for so long that it is as the air we breathe. I doubt if we could survive in an atmosphere of peace and security. But I'm not going to keep you here, lad, though that was my intention at first."

Owen was surprised and disappointed. But O'Cahane continued, "It's a rough life we lead, though that is not my reason for sending you away. You'll be safer elsewhere."

He walked towards the entrance to the cave, where he gave the familiar signal. In a moment Owen heard footsteps and Sean came in. As he saluted O'Cahane smartly, he gave Owen a quick smile.

"You're going to stay with Sean and his mother, Owen. You two will not be sorry to be together again. I count on both of you to keep out of danger. Now, be off." Silently following Sean up and over the hill above the cave, Owen had no time to be sad. He was too busy trying to walk as quickly and quietly as Sean, who was as good as any of O'Cahane's men. But he alone among them seemed to be enjoying himself.

When they came to the foot of the hill, the trees were farther apart. Soon they were in open pasture land, and Sean waited for Owen to join him.

"The sheep used to keep this nibbled close to the ground," he explained as they waded through the high grass and small bushes which brushed against their knees. "But there haven't been any since my father and brothers went away."

"Why don't you come to France when I go?" Owen asked, partly in response to the sorrow in Sean's voice.

"And what would become of my mother if I did that? I was left behind to look after her and that I'll do while I can. We're luckier than most, for the O'Briens still hold title to this land and we are their tenants—for how long, who knows?" Sean shrugged. "They do say that William will take all the lands that are left to the Irish and give them to his Dutchmen, or to the English who brought him over, curse them."

Across the fields Owen could see a two-story stone house backed up against a hillock where the trees began again. Smoke rose invitingly from the chimney, for clouds had covered the sun and there was a damp chill in the air. He would have quickened his pace had Sean not stopped him.

"Before we get to the house, I must explain that my mother does not know who you are. All she has been told is that you're a lad O'Cahane wants hidden and that's enough for her. If it wasn't for the help he and his men gave us when we came back from Cork, we'd not have lived through the winter. She knows you are Owen, but she doesn't know your last name. Should you meet any others while you're here, you're the son of my Uncle Nick, who lives beyond Ennis."

"I'll remember."

"Now, I'll race you to the house." Sean was off, his long legs carrying him quickly over the ground and to their goal several paces ahead of Owen.

"Here he is!" Sean called as Owen came to the door. "Here's our guest, Mother."

As the two boys entered, Mrs. O'Kelly turned from the broad fireplace to greet them. "It's welcome you are, lad, since you're a friend of O'Cahane's. Though I take it ill that I'm to know no more of you than that." Her cheerful face belied her grumbling.

Owen took her hand. "Now isn't it my aunt you are?" he asked softly. "I'd take it ill indeed if you refused to acknowledge me, for I'm proud to be called your nephew."

Mrs. O'Kelly beamed. "You're a good lad and a clever one, and it's gladly I'll call you my nephew. Now Sean show Owen his room, but be quick about it, or dinner will be ready before you are." She bustled back to the fireplace. The smell of steaming bacon and vegetables came from the pot oven. It made Owen hungry, as he followed Sean upstairs and into a small chamber. A narrow bed, made up with home-woven blankets and coarse linen sheets, and a straight chair were all that the room contained. It looked wonderful to Owen, for he had not slept in a proper bed since he had left Dublin. The one window, he noticed, looked out over the way they had come.

"Well, and have you never seen such a room before?" Sean teased.

"It's been a long time since I have. I think O'Cahane did me a kindness in sending me here, though I wanted to stay with him."

"Aye, it's better than the cave. I sleep across from you, Mother's room is downstairs. Let's go."

In the pleasant kitchen the meal was laid on the long table in the center. Owen sat down before a plate of the bacon and vegetables he had been smelling. There was white bread and butter, a pitcher of milk and, at each place, a pewter mug, knife and spoon, and a linen napkin. Looking across, he saw Sean's impish grin.

"Our guest isn't used to such grandeur," he said, in a feigned aside to his mother.

"That I don't believe," she replied, looking keenly at Owen. "He's gently bred, I'm sure, even if I'm to know nothing about him."

Both boys laughed.

"I'm your nephew from beyond Ennis, remember."

"Yes," she said. "And if you were my nephew, wouldn't I put out the best that I have, though I keep it hidden most of the time for fear the English thieves might happen by and see it."

"This afternoon," Sean told her, "Owen and I are going fishing, so with luck we'll have trout for supper."

Owen was pleased. He had feared that Sean would have to work in the cultivated fields that lay around the house.

When they started out on their fishing trip, Sean explained that they were going a roundabout way, for he had messages to deliver in places where O'Cahane did not wish to send one of his men. In fact, the fishing was only an excuse for such errands which Sean frequently did. In exchange O'Cahane would send a man now and then to help with the farm work. It was a welcome arrangement to Sean who hated the long drudgery in the fields.

Three times Owen waited in a secluded spot while Sean pursued the business which had been entrusted to him. When they came to the stream where they were to fish, Sean left Owen for a longer interval than before. Owen hooked two good-sized trout while he waited.

When Sean returned, he asked Owen, "The wolf hound called Brian is yours, isn't he?"

"Yes! Did you see him? Where is he?"

"He's up there. What a grand dog he is!"

"Do you think I could see him, Sean? Perhaps from a spot where I couldn't be seen?" Owen looked with longing in the direction from which Sean had come.

"It wouldn't be possible at all. I shouldn't have mentioned seeing him. It was only that I wished O'Cahane had left him with me."

"I'd like you to have him, Sean. Perhaps after I've gone, you can. I'll speak to O'Cahane."

"Thanks. I'd be glad to have him." Sean was looking at the trout Owen had caught. "That'll be enough. It's late. We'd better be getting back."

Traveling through woods and fields by ways Sean knew, they came to a place where they had to cross the Ennis road. Suddenly Sean held up a warning hand. Getting behind a tree trunk, he motioned to Owen to do the same. In a minute Owen heard the sound of horses' hooves and the creak of saddle leather. Looking out cautiously, he saw a troop of English cavalry cantering along the road. When the last sound of their passing had died on the still air, Sean and Owen came out of hiding and hastily crossed the road, seeking the shelter of the trees on the other side.

Once they were well away from the road, Sean spoke, a note of alarm in his voice, "What do you suppose that means? It looks as if they were on the hunt for someone."

Owen made no answer as he wondered if Sean knew that two nights ago just such a troop had searched the house at Cloona, while Owen and Father D'Arcy hid in the secret room. And the troop which had passed was coming from Ennis. In spite of Sean's precautions, Owen had felt no sense of danger all afternoon in the woods. But there was danger for him anywhere in Ireland, as Patrick had said.

Sean took a roundabout way towards home. When

they were in sight of it, but still screened by trees, he stopped.

"I think you'd better wait here, Owen. I'll see if all is calm before you come to the house."

"Perhaps I'd better not come at all," Owen suggested. "I wouldn't want harm to come to your mother because of me."

"And what would you do?" asked Sean impatiently. "Stay here for the night? And if O'Cahane should send for you, what would I tell him? Remember I have his orders to keep you at my house. Wait for me here. Give me one of the fish so that I will have an excuse for my afternoon in the woods if I meet anyone. If you hear anyone coming, start walking towards the house. If someone stops you, remember you're my cousin."

Sean went off, moving quietly through the woods, then out into the open fields. His shadow lay long across the grass when he paused for a moment before going indoors. Owen watched impatiently until he saw Sean come out. But instead of coming back towards Owen, Sean disappeared around the corner of the house. While Owen was wondering what that meant, he heard the familiar curlew's call coming from the direction which Sean had taken. From the distance came the answering signal. Owen watched and listened, but he could see no movement in the fields nor hear anything but the sleepy calls of small birds and the rustling of the leaves. After a long time he caught distinctly the sound of twigs cracking, as if someone were walking in the woods behind him. Remembering Sean's instructions, he started towards the fields. He heard nothing more until a hand grabbed his shoulder. He stopped breathing as he looked around into Sean's laughing face.

"I really didn't set out to frighten you, Owen. When I got home, I found a message and had to get in touch with the rapparees immediately. Then I took the quickest way back to you. It wasn't until you started walking that I realized you didn't know I was the one coming behind you."

"I started walking as you had said to do. When you touched me, I jumped. I hadn't even thought of being afraid before that."

"You certainly showed no fear. Come, let's get home. All is serene there, and Mother is waiting for that other trout."

When they entered the kitchen, Mrs. O'Kelly took the fish from Owen.

"A poor showing for an afternoon's work," she said tartly. "One trout apiece!"

When Owen would have denied this, Sean's hand on his elbow reminded him of the real reason for the fishing trip.

"Hurry up now!" Mrs. O'Kelly exclaimed. "The fish will be cooked while you stand there."

Owen's appetite for supper was not as good as it had been at noon. Once more he was aware of the dangerous position he was in, only a few miles from Hugh. It was not impossible that the English troop were looking for him. They might even come here. But the rapparees were on guard, he reassured himself.

Nevertheless, he went to bed reluctantly, sure that he would not sleep. But he must have dozed off, for suddenly he was aware of being wide awake, hearing his name called. He listened, every muscle tense. There it was again. "Owen Bourke! Owen Bourke!"

Instantly he was on his feet. There was a heavy thud against the house wall, followed by a sound he could not identify. He was almost at the window when he drew back. Moonlight shone through the glass. He dared not look out. For it was no friend who called his name, he felt certain. He hurried across the hall to Sean's room. The bed was empty. From the open window Owen saw a tree branch within easy reach. It looked heavy enough to carry a boy's weight. Had Sean swung himself out on it? Was it he who was under Owen's window? Was this another of his jokes? No, Owen could not believe it was. Dearly as Sean loved a joke, he would not risk Owen's full name. Wherever he had gone, it was not to the other side of the house. With that certainty Owen realized that he was alone and in danger. He ought to get out of the house, by Sean's route.

Walking lightly on his bare feet, he went back to his own room. Again he heard his name called faintly, followed by that other sound. This time he knew what it was—the muffled roar of a muzzled dog. Brian! He had been used to trace Owen. His heart pounded as he pulled on the frieze trousers and coat. Hastily he rearranged the bedclothes. He must leave no sign that he had been in the room. He dared not put on the stiff brogans, lest their heavy tread wake Mrs. O'Kelly. His caller was still beneath the window for "Owen Bourke!" came faintly again, followed by Brian's now-unmistakable growl. Owen's fingers fumbled in his haste to tie the leather lacings of his brogans together. At last he succeeded and swung them around his neck, as Sean had taught him when they had forded a stream.

Back in Sean's room, Owen reached out the window. He could grip the branch with both hands as he stood there. First climbing to the sill, he swung out clear of the house. The branch dipped with his weight, but he was well above the ground as, hand over hand, he pulled himself towards the trunk. He breathed deeply when he rested his body against it, taking some of the weight from his aching wrists. With one hand he reached for a higher branch. Looking up, he could see a notch where the trunk separated. He climbed to the notch and found he could sit there quite comfortably and watch the house. He was hardly settled when he saw a stooped figure, holding the dog on a tight leash, come around the corner.

Owen held his breath. The window directly under the one by which he had escaped must be in Mrs. O'Kelly's room. She would surely be wakened if his name were called. To his relief, the man went by the window holding Brian's head low. He was trying for a scent which would lead away from the house, Owen realized. Soon man and dog disappeared around the side of the house. What would be the next move Owen could not guess, but he must plan what he would do.

His first thought was to stay in the tree until Sean returned. That could be dangerous if the man were still around, for Sean would require some warning. Yet Owen's instinct rejected the idea of returning to the house. The farther away from it he could get, the safer both he and Mrs. O'Kelly would be. If he could get to the top of the hill behind him, he could see over the roof of the house. Cautiously he let himself down to the ground. It was hard-packed beneath his feet. Gratefully, he realized that he was on a path which led uphill. In his stocking feet it was not difficult to follow. At the top it levelled off and turned along the ridge, where the trees grew too thickly to see the land below. Owen walked along slowly, watching for a place where the foliage thinned. He had not gone far when he came to a spot where he could look down on the side wall of the house, the field in front of it, and the black woods on the hill beyond. There were no moving figures to be seen. Owen guessed that the man with Brian was again beneath the chamber window.

Owen dared not go back. Since his identity was known or suspected, his presence would be a danger to Mrs. O'Kelly. He must go on, though he did not know where the path might lead. O'Cahane's cave was somewhere beyond those fields and woods. Owen doubted his ability to find the cave by circling around the farm and did not know what road or dwelling lay between. The only thing to do was to keep on the path, increasing the distance between himself and Sean's home. Other than that, he could make no plan.

Abruptly, he came to the end of the path and the woods. Screened by the last row of trees, he could see that the land fell away in a steep slope from where he stood. There might be a road at the bottom, but the moon was too low in the sky to light the hollow. Some instinct told him that he should go no farther. Once off the ridge, he would be lost in the darkness below. He must wait here on the chance that Sean might return this way. If he did not, Owen decided he would have to signal the rapparees.

Even as he came to this decision, he heard a noise behind him. Quickly he stepped off the path and got behind a tree. Something was coming towards him. Before he could decide who or what, he saw Brian, his head close to the ground, pulling on the leash. The man at the other end was bent low as he was dragged along by the dog. In a minute they would be upon Owen. There was no place to hide. He grabbed his brogans from around his neck. After twisting the lacing around his wrist, he rolled the uppers down until he had the shoes firmly gripped in one hand, soles out, ready to strike.

Brian gave a yelp of joy as he leaped on his master. "Down Brian," Owen commanded, grabbing the leash. With a quick tug he brought the man holding it to the ground, then hit him hard on the back of the head with the brogans. Quieting Brian with one hand, Owen got down on one knee beside his victim. Dropping the brogans, Owen reached out to touch a bony shoulder. There was no response, no movement. Brian pushed his nose under Owen's outstretched hand.

"What shall I do, Brian?" Owen laid his cheek against the dog's soft fur. He did not want to leave the man there. He might be dead, but dead or alive, someone would be looking for him.

A hand grasped Owen's shoulder. Frightened, Owen struggled to break the hold, while Brian growled.

"Keep that dog quiet." It was Sean's voice and Owen laid a restraining hand on Brian.

Sean gave a low whistle. In a moment two men appeared on the path. One held out his hand to Owen.

"Go with him," Sean ordered, taking the leash Owen still held. Though Brian whimpered, he obeyed Owen's command to stay, as boy and man took off into the woods. Owen had no time to think as he was rushed along the rough ground by the strong hand holding him. Soon they came to a clearing where two horses were tethered. The rapparee silently gave Owen a hand up onto one. Mounting the other, the man started off, Owen's horse following.

Owen was suddenly so tired that he had to struggle to keep his seat. That was all he had to do, for his horse needed no guidance. Before long they were back on familiar ground near the entrance to the cave. When the horses halted, O'Cahane stepped out of the shadows and practically lifting Owen out of the saddle, led him up to the cave.

Seating Owen in the armchair, O'Cahane asked, "Why did you leave the house?"

Owen told him of the voice calling his name, of discovering Sean's absence, and of his fear that harm might come to Mrs. O'Kelly if he did not get away.

"You did well, Owen. It was I who sent Sean out thinking you were well guarded, but Tom Nance slipped through with the dog. He's a half-witted old chap who lives at the farm where I left Brian."

"Do you think I killed him?" Owen was suddenly afraid, remembering the crumpled, inert heap on the ground.

"I'm sure you didn't. He was just stunned. When he

comes to, he'll not know what hit him. Denis is standing by, but he'll make sure Nance doesn't see him. When Nance recovers, he'll have to report his failure to the traitor who sent him. Tomorrow we'll find out who that was."

"How did Sean happen along just then?"

"When he returned home to find you gone, he gave the rapparee's signal, knowing some were near. He could tell you had gone out the window, so assumed you had taken the path up the hill and went after you when Denis and Dominik arrived. But where did you learn to hit a man that way?"

"I was never taught. I just had to do something."

"You did well," O'Cahane said again. "Old Tom will never know that he found you."

"My shoes!" Owen exclaimed. "I left them there on the ground."

"They'll be recovered, never fear. Nance won't get a chance to carry them off."

"Sir, what do you think this is all about? Is it Hugh Bourke's doing?"

"I believe it is, to some extent. He arrived at Cloona this afternoon with quite an escort. He's in high favor with the enemy, no doubt about that. What I fear is that, in spite of our care, you've been linked with Father D'Arcy and that he's the real object of the search."

"What about Sean and his mother? Will the searchers look for me there?"

"I'm sure they will, though not before dawn. They'll stay safe and warm during the dark hours. But don't worry. The O'Kellys will be a match for anyone who comes questioning. Now you must get some sleep, Owen, for when night falls again we start for Dunbeg. Please God you'll be safe on a boat for France before two days have passed."

"And Patrick?"

"Patrick will join us on the way, I promise."

CHAPTER FOURTEEN

Within the cave, Owen moved restlessly. Cut off from the daylight, he had no idea of time, but it seemed long hours since one of the rapparees had brought him an oaten cake and some milk. O'Cahane he had not seen since the night before. The man who had brought him food had said only that he was not to leave the cave. A slight sound in the passage alerted him. Sean entered the rockwalled room.

"So you heard me coming? I hoped to surprise you, but you're getting too smart."

"Is everything all right at your house? Did anyone come looking for me there?"

"Aye, two soldiers waked us at dawn. But my mother had half persuaded them there was no one in the place but her and me, even before they made the search. They went away convinced Brian had led them on a wild goose chase."

"And did O'Cahane find out who set Nance and Brian on me?"

"Aye, but he'll maybe tell you himself. I've spent the morning in the fields as if that was the way I did every day, until O'Cahane signalled that it was safe for me to come here. My mother was worrying about what you'd get to eat, so she sent you this." Sean brought out from under his shirt a round loaf of bread, carefully wrapped in a clean napkin. It had been split and buttered while hot. Owen bit into it eagerly.

Sean grinned at him. "She'll be pleased that you enjoyed it. I've tried to persuade O'Cahane to let me ride to the coast, but he says 'No.' I've got to remain at home since suspicion has been directed there. I had to take a roundabout way to get to see you at all."

"I'm so glad you came, Sean. I worried about your mother. Wasn't she surprised when she found me gone?"

"Not too much. She's used to the ways of the rapparees. I told her as soon as I got back, in case we had visitors."

"Tell her I'm sorry to have left so abruptly and say my thanks for me, please, Sean."

"That I will, though she needs no thanks for what she did. O'Cahane's request would be enough. Then she took quite a fancy to you, while wondering who you were, of course."

"Perhaps you can tell her after I've gone. What time of day is it? Cooped up here I don't even know if the sun shines."

"It doesn't. It's afternoon now of a gray day with fog hiding the hills. You've a wet night ahead."

"All the better." O'Cahane's voice startled them. "The soldiers have been everywhere today, but they'll be looking for a warm, dry place to spend the night, I warrant. Now you'd best be off, Sean. Don't forget the bag of meal you went to fetch from the miller. Let no one see you till you're near home."

Sean nodded and saluted O'Cahane. He raised his left arm in a gesture of farewell to Owen and was gone.

"I wish he were coming with me all the way to Maryland," Owen said.

"Someday he may follow you there," was the unexpected reply. "This time Patrick goes, and two of my men as well. 'Tis all the sloop will hold."

"More will come later?" Owen asked.

"Yes. Two go now. Perhaps it will be four, the next time a boat sails for France. By next spring they'll all be gone to fight and die for some foreign king. A better fate, perhaps, than to be hunted down by the Dutchman's troops and die a criminal's death."

"And you?" Owen asked, remembering the bitter tirade against Sarsfield and those who had followed him.

With a wry face, the rapparee leader answered, "Aye, when the others are over the water, I'll be going to France too. I'd as soon stay here, but the kind of war I've waged can serve no purpose now that hope of an Irish victory is gone. It could only make worse the lot of those who are left. When the time comes, Sean and his mother will go with me."

"You will join the Irish Brigade?" Owen asked.

"You can't picture me a regular soldier?" O'Cahane smiled, as he said, "I can't myself. I might volunteer for New France. I've no doubt the French king could use me there."

178

"Why not come to Maryland?"

"Why not, indeed? But that's all a long way off."
O'Cahane stood up. "I've a few orders to give before we
ride. Get some sleep now. You've a long night ahead."
He left the cave.

Alone, Owen thought about Maryland. There, in that
new country, the rapparees would be more valuable and
happier than in the strict discipline of the Irish Brigade.
Perhaps, when he was ready to go, at least some of
O'Cahane's men would go, too, plus Sean and his mother, his father, and brothers. Mrs. O'Kelly would be a
better companion for his mother than Anna. Somehow
his mother would join him when the time came, he knew.
Monsieur Castillon would be the one to make that arrangement. Owen drifted off to sleep.

He was awakened by O'Cahane's hand on his arm.

"Time to go."

Owen was on his feet as O'Cahane handed him a
cloak. "You'll need this, for the night is chill." He took
the candle from its stand to light their way. The mist was
like a wall at the cave's entrance. The candle extinguished, Owen had to keep one hand on the rock while
following O'Cahane along the now familiar path. They
were going down the hill. When they came to the clearing, Owen could see other gray shapes. He was guided
to a horse, and reins were placed in his hand. He mounted, sensing that the horseman nearest him was O'Cahane. Owen could make out three others in the clearing.
As he did, one of them rode off. Soon the curlew's call
was repeated twice. The answering signal sounded far
away.

Leaning close, O'Cahane whispered, "Follow me." Owen was aware that the other two in the clearing were remaining. He guessed that they would wait for another signal.

When they came to the end of the bog, the horses stopped and Owen knew that O'Cahane was looking carefully to left and right, though even his keen eyes could see little through the enveloping mist. Then the rapparee leader gave the familiar signal, the answer coming from across the bog. He turned his horse's head to the right towards the mountains and the sea. The other way lay Cloona, and this time Owen knew there would be no coming back. There was a lump in his throat, and the fog hid his tears. They had not gone far when the horses turned into a grove of trees. Under the dripping branches, two mounted men waited. One rode up to Owen.

"I'm coming with you as I promised, Master Owen." It was only a whisper, but there was no mistaking Patrick's voice. Owen silently reached out to grasp the extended hand. There was comfort in the touch. In a moment, as if at a signal he had not seen or heard, Patrick's hand was withdrawn as he rode forward.

Owen remained where he was, O'Cahane by his side. In a few minutes two horsemen rode in among the trees. After a whispered conference with them, O'Cahane turned his horse towards the road, beckoning Owen to follow. Shivering, he pulled his cloak about him, for the chill mist penetrated his clothing. The horses were slowed to a walk. At this pace they would never get to the sea.

O'Cahane's hand over Owen's brought both horses to a halt. Leaning over so that his mouth was close to Owen's ear, he whispered, "We leave the road here. Give your horse her head. She will follow me. The two men we left at the clearing may come up with us. No one else will pass this point."

Owen could make out the dim outline of another horse and rider who remained motionless as they turned off the road. The horses were picking their footing carefully, so that Owen knew they were again crossing a bog. The enveloping mist pressed his eyelids down so that he could hardly keep awake. A wet branch brushed his face as he felt the horse's pace quicken.

The change of pace roused him. All at once he was aware of the sound of hooves behind him. For a moment he was frightened. Then remembering O'Cahane's words, he knew that it was the rapparees he heard. As they rode on and on, weariness pressed down again. Owen felt he could not sit erect in the saddle much longer. But these men of O'Cahane's were as tireless as their leader. They must not see him slump. In spite of his efforts, his head began to droop, to be brought up abruptly when his horse almost stopped, then slowly began a steep climb. Owen had to grasp the saddle to save himself from falling backwards. It was a long slow climb over rough ground, and the jolting kept Owen awake. He thought he smelled burning brush as his horse moved forward eagerly. In a moment they were on a ridge, then dropped into a hollow where the mist was thinner. And there was a small fire burning. Patrick came towards them.

"How did you stand the long ride, Patrick?"

"I was stiff enough when at last we arrived here. Come to the fire, lad. Your clothes are damp and you must be hungry and tired. We've come a long way and we'll be starting off again, I've no doubt, as soon as the horses are rested."

Owen blinked against the glare. The smell of bacon, mingled with the odor of burning wood, came to his nostrils. He shifted his head to get out of the direct rays of the sun, then opened his eyes. He saw Patrick by the fire.

"So you're awake, lad, I thought the smell of food might rouse you. You must be hungry, for it's many a long hour since you ate. You fell asleep before you were well off your horse last night."

"What time is it?" Owen sat up, rubbing his eyes. "I thought we were going on last night?"

"Aye, that was the plan. But another rapparee followed us here, and O'Cahane and his men rode off with him at dawn."

As he talked, Patrick was removing the bacon from the fire. Placing a slice on a large oaten cake, he handed it to Owen. After eating a few mouthfuls, Owen asked:

"Where did they go? When will they be back? What did O'Cahane say when he left?"

"One question at a time, lad." Patrick was busy scattering the ashes and digging into the damp earth to bury them. "You should know that O'Cahane wastes no words. He said only that I was to wait here with you until they returned. He did also say that I could light a small fire when the sun was up. It's good I've more patience than you, for I've been awake the whole time, and the day's half over now."

"I hoped we'd be safe on board a boat before this."

"Now don't fret yourself, lad. O'Cahane has undertaken to get you on a vessel bound for France. He will not fail."

Owen was silent for he knew Patrick was right. Wherever O'Cahane had gone, he would return in his own time. Meanwhile, there was nothing to do but wait. He put his hand on his coat where he could feel the documents hidden between the frieze and lining. Nothing must happen now to prevent him getting them safely out of Ireland. A chuckle from Patrick surprised him. Looking around he could see no cause for mirth.

"I was just thinking," Patrick explained, "I'd like to have seen Hugh Bourke's face when he found me gone this morning."

"You haven't told me how you got away, nor what happened when Hugh came."

There was a complacent smile on Patrick's face as he began: "Getting away was easy enough. There were soldiers all around, to be sure; and Hugh giving them orders to go this way and that and to bring you back without fail. The courtyard was full of them, but I just walked into the stable and out the door at the rear. None of them had discovered the path there. So I went along until I came to the place where Dominick was waiting. Then I mounted the horse he had for me and off we rode. I've no doubt I wasn't missed until this morning."

"Did Hugh suspect I'd been at Cloona?" Owen asked.

"Indeed he thought to find you there when he came." Patrick's voice lingered with relish over the words. "Didn't he come riding into the courtyard with an escort of soldiers and never stopped until he arrived at the door of my cottage, calling 'Patrick! Patrick!' as lordly as you please. Oh, I was very lame that day. I could hardly hobble to the door when he called. And him waiting more impatient than you are now."

For Owen was snapping a twig in tense fingers.

"When finally I got there, he was sitting his horse with the skirt of his scarlet coat spread out just so, the plumes on his big hat nodding, and a black frown on his face.

" 'Bring out the boy!' he commanded, as if he were the king himself.

" 'The boy!' I repeated, as if I'd never heard of a boy before. 'Oh, it is Gavin you mean, sir? For he's with his mother in the village, though I'd have him here, had I known you were coming.'

" 'It's not Gavin I mean and you know it.' He rapped that out like a drill master.

" 'Then I don't know what boy you mean, sir,' I answered, all bewildered." Owen had to laugh at Patrick's expression.

"Then he got off the horse and came up to me, speaking so low the others couldn't hear him.

" 'I know your loyalty to your old master," Patrick,' he said gentlelike, 'but I'm your master now and I know well that Owen Bourke is here.'

" 'Master Owen!' I cried.

" 'Not so loud, Patrick,' he warned, leaning towards

me, 'My men don't know he's the boy I'm looking for. I'm only trying to protect him, Patrick,' he went on wheedlingly. 'It's known he was in Dublin with the priest who's sought as a spy. It will go hard with him if the English take him!'

" 'Master Owen in Dublin, you say.' My tone would have convinced an angel it was the first I'd heard it. 'So that's where he's been. And is he still there, do you think?' "

Owen had moved closer to Patrick, and sitting with arms clasped around his knees, waited for the rest of the story.

" 'No he's not and well you know it,' He'd stopped being persuasive. 'He's here somewhere and it will go hard with you, Patrick Hogan, if you don't bring him out. For I'll find him.' By this time he had me by the coat and his face close to mine.

" 'Find him, if you can, Mr. Hugh,' I replied, 'but if you do, it'll be a surprise to me.'

" 'All right, Patrick! But remember my words.'

"Then he went back to the soldiers and, at his command, they scattered, two coming in immediately to search the cottage. And I stood aside for them, as if, as was so, it mattered not a bit to me. They looked all around the kitchen, then went up to the loft where there was nothing to be found as you know. Others were in the stable, prodding in the hay and tossing it onto the floor. And they went through the offices as well, till they swore there was nobody anywhere about. Though there were half a dozen places a man might hide that they didn't see at all. But no matter.

"Then Hugh himself led them into the house, while I went about getting my supper. In a minute I heard my name called as Master Hugh came stamping across the courtyard. And, if his face had been black before, the scowl on it now frightened the horses, so they shied and reared up, and some soldiers had to come running out to hold them.

"And I came to the door, anxious to please, though I couldn't move very fast that day with the lameness.

" 'Patrick!' he bellowed. 'What's the meaning of this?'

" 'The meaning of what?' I asked.

" 'The condition that house is in,' he stormed.

" 'As to that I wouldn't know,' I answered, looking him full in the face. 'For your orders were that no one was to go into it, when you left last winter. So nobody has.'

"It was almost worth the ruin of Cloona to see his face at that moment, lad. I wouldn't repeat the names he called me, but all I said was that I had obeyed his instructions. Finally he threw up his arms in despair. Then he called the two servants who had been left standing by the horses all the while the soldiers were searching for you. They looked none too pleased at the orders he gave them: to have the place in readiness by nightfall—and the sun way down in the sky already.

"The sergeant came out to tell him they had searched every nook and cranny of the place. He was covered with dust. He'd been in every closet, poked under beds and behind curtains. There was no one hidden in the house, he swore."

"So my fine cousin Hugh wasn't pleased with the condition of the place. And he'd like to protect me from the English, would he? God keep me from his protection."

"Amen!" O'Cahane's voice startled them.

Owen jumped to his feet, expecting a reprimand, but he was greeted pleasantly.

"All's well, but we must start immediately. My horse is up on the ridge with Dominick and Dermot. We've only a few more miles to go to where the sloop lies anchored."

"And are we riding into Dunbeg in broad daylight?" Owen could not refrain from asking.

O'Cahane, who was stamping down the earth where the fire had been, looked annoyed. Hastily Owen busied himself saddling his horse and Patrick's. They mounted. O'Cahane, on foot, led the way up the ridge to where the two men waited. Leaping into the saddle, the rapparee leader started off. Owen followed, then Patrick. Behind him the other two rode, all without a word being exchanged.

Their path went steeply down the side of the mountain. The slope was so heavily wooded that Owen could see nothing but the next bend. The descent was long and slow. Owen guessed they had been riding at least an hour before the land flattened out and the path widened. The horses ran along the level track. Owen was cheered by the swift motion and by the knowledge that he would soon be out of the reach of Hugh Bourke. There was a freedom in the very air that blew against his cheek, damp with a touch of the sea.

They climbed another small hill. At the summit O'Cahane halted, motioning the others to come up to him.

Below them, they could see a small inlet, where a sloop lay at anchor. Owen was amazed. Surely that small boat could never sail to France.

As if in answer to his thought, O'Cahane spoke: "Ten times in the past year Captain Mongan has made the voyage. He's the best sailor on this coast. I leave you in safe hands when I deliver you to him. We walk from here."

Dermot and Dominick produced ropes with which they expertly tied the horses, so that they could crop the grass while they waited. For whom, Owen wondered, for O'Cahane could hardly lead the four horses back the long miles they had come. But he asked no more questions.

Motioning the others to go ahead, O'Cahane walked beside Owen as they started downhill.

"We couldn't go to Dunbeg," he explained, "because the soldiers were watching there. That's what took me off last night. I had to get word to the sloop to put in here instead. They certainly were leaving no stone unturned to find you, Owen."

"Does that mean they're still looking for Father D'Arcy?"

"I hope so. We know he got safely to Dublin. Beyond that we expected no word, unless he needed us. It was best that way. But he left some papers with Bart Flaherty to deliver to you when you were sailing for France. Let's sit down here for a minute."

There was a small outcropping of rock above the sandy beach where Patrick and the others waited.

"There's time yet, for the sloop will go out on the ebb

tide," O'Cahane continued when they were seated. He took from his coat an oilskin package, which he handed to Owen.

"Give this to Monsieur Castillon when you get to Paris. He will know where to deliver it."

As Owen took the package, he thought of those other papers safe inside his coat. But for the man beside him he would never have brought them safely this far. Falteringly, Owen tried to speak his thanks.

O'Cahane brushed the words aside. "All I want from you, Owen, is that you remember what I say to you now. It may sound strange coming from me, but I beg of you do not dream of returning here one day. You are young, life lies before you. Make it a good one in some other land. Remember the home of your youth with affection, but when the sloop puts out to sea, look not back."

He rose, drawing Owen up with him. Silently they walked to where Dominick and Dermot had already launched a curragh which had been drawn up on the beach. Patrick took O'Cahane's hand, then climbed aboard. Owen followed, too moved to speak. O'Cahane gave the boat a shove, as the two men used their oars to push the boat off the beach. Owen felt the lift as it floated on the water. Raising his hand once, the rapparee leader turned to take the path up the hill.

They were beside the sloop now. A rope was thrown over the side, and one by one they climbed the ladder to the deck.

As the boat slipped out to sea on the tide, only a faint breeze puffing the sails, Owen looked towards the hill where, he imagined, O'Cahane stood. Raising his hand in salute to the invisible watcher, he turned away remembering the words, "Look not back."

Owen looked to the west, toward a new land.